DREAMS OF SHIPS, DREAMS OF JULIA

AT SEA WITH THE *MONITOR* AND THE *MERRIMACK*—VIRGINIA, 1862

Young American Series #2

By

Maureen Stack Sappéy

WHITE MANE KIDS

This White Mane Books publication
was printed by
Beidel Printing House, Inc.
63 West Burd Street
Shippensburg, PA 17257-0152 USA

In respect for the scholarship contained herein, the acid-free paper used in this book meets the guidelines for permanence and durability of the Committee on Production Guidelines for Book Longevity of the Council on Library Resources.

For a complete list of available publications
please write
White Mane Books
Division of White Mane Publishing Company, Inc.
P.O. Box 152
Shippensburg, PA 17257-0152 USA

Library of Congress Cataloging-in-Publication Data

Sappey, Maureen Stack, 1952–
    Dreams of ships, dreams of Julia : at sea with the Monitor and the Merrimack--Virginia, 1862 / by Maureen Stack Sappéy.
        p.   cm. -- (Young American series : #2)
    Summary: A young engineering student leaves Harvard to help build an ironclad ship to defend the Union against Confederate naval forces, and is subsequently blinded in the Battle of Hampton Roads.
    ISBN 1-57249-134-5 (alk. paper)
    1. United States--History--Civil War, 1861–1865--Naval operations--Juvenile fiction. [1. United States--History--Civil War, 1861–1865--Naval operations--Fiction. 2. Monitor (Ironclad)--Fiction. 3. Merrimack (Frigate)--Fiction. 4. Blind--Fiction. 5. Physically handicapped--Fiction.] I. Title. II. Series.
PZ7.S2388Dr   1998
[Fic]--DC21   98-3858
                                                                   CIP
                                                                   A C

With great love, I dedicate this book to my son, John James Sappéy, an engineering student at St. Francis College, Pennsylvania, who, unknowingly, served as a model for the character of James.

Contents

Chapter One

Dreams. All my life I dreamed about ships. When I was a small boy I dreamed of building graceful sail-ships that skimmed across the oceans of our world. When I was a school boy I dreamed of building boiler-driven ships that steamed to exotic ports. And when I was fourteen years of age I entered Harvard to study engineering. For three years I studied with fierce determination to make those dream ships a reality.

One night last August, I was at my desk copying naval designs from a book written by that celebrated engineer, Mr. John Ericsson. The gas lamp near my head burned bright and hot, for I had been sketching his designs since supper. I welcomed the quiet of my room. The student I shared chambers with was away visiting his family in Washington—a very important family—for that student was none other than Robert Lincoln, President Lincoln's eldest son.

I can't say that Robert and I were close friends. Although we shared rooms, we rarely sought out each other's company. We had no common interests and usually he studied at the library, for he avoided lugging heavy books of law across the greens of the campus. I preferred privacy when I studied, so I welcomed his long absences.

Some of the students envied my sharing rooms with President Lincoln's son, but their envy would have disappeared if they had known Robert as I did. He tended to be close-mouthed like a monk under the vow of silence, and on occasion when he did speak, he never mentioned his family. In particular, I disliked his sullen avoidance of any mention of his father.

However, that night in August, Robert spoke at length about his father, President Abraham Lincoln, and what he told me changed my life forever. His words brought my dream ships to reality, and for a few brief months, I lived my dream.

* * * * *

It happened thus . . . in the hour before midnight Robert came through the door carrying his luggage and a dripping umbrella. He dropped both on his desk and then turned to me with a peculiar expression on his face.

I suppose ladies would find him attractive. He is tall enough and dark of hair, but his scornful eyes are piercing, off-putting. His arrogant manner might impress his future law clients, but his attitude will never win him close friends. That night, however, Robert seemed less arrogant, less haughty, and I saw at once that he was sorely troubled.

I poured hot coffee and gave him a cup. He drank it down without saying a word, but then, unable to keep his troubles to himself, he blurted out, "James, the Confederates have resurrected one of the Union's old ships, the *Merrimack*. They have raised her from under the water, drained the mud from her hull and engines, and put her in dry dock at their naval base in Norfolk, Virginia. Even as we speak the *Merrimack* is being covered with iron plates and bars. The Confederates are changing her from a wooden ship into an ironclad ship—a ramming ironclad that will be afloat within months."

I understood at once the import of Robert's words. The Confederates were building a monster, an unstoppable monster of iron with strength enough to destroy our Union's entire fleet of wooden ships. And, if our fleet was destroyed, Mr. Lincoln's blockade of Southern ports would end and foreign nations could ship in the food and weapons and cloth that the Confederacy desperately needs for her armies. The ironclad, *Merrimack*, was a monstrous threat to our Union. She had to be destroyed!

In my mind's eye, I could picture the Confederate's ironclad already afloat, already ramming, crushing, and destroying our ships and a fear I've never known washed over me. I clenched my fist and snapped my pen in half. I stared down at the slivers of wood in my hand. The Confederate's ironclad could destroy each and every wooden ship as easily as I had broken the pen.

I waited in silence to hear more of Robert's terrible news. For awhile he said nothing else as he paced around the room, tearing off his coat and gloves and throwing them onto the floor. After some time he dragged over a chair and placing it squarely before me he said, "Three days ago I accompanied my father to a meeting of his Naval Board—three commodores and father's Secretary of the Navy, Mr. Gideon Welles, were amongst the gentlemen. The meeting had one purpose—to decide if the Union should build its own ironclad."

Robert paused, his brow creasing as he said, "All of the gentlemen were agitated, except for Mr. Welles; he was, as usual, calm and quiet, a man of dignified composure.

"My father's Secretary of State, Mr. Seward, was not calm. He stood during much of the meeting at a window, staring down at the Potomac River. Then, like a flash of heated lightning, he turned to us and shouted that Washington was doomed! Mr. Seward has convinced himself that the Confederates intend to float their ironclad up the Potomac and shell the Executive Mansion and all government buildings that edge the river. He expressed no faith in our Navy Department or the Secretary. More than once he shook his fist at Mr. Welles and demanded to know if he had a plan to protect my father from certain death."

Robert sat down heavily and the troubled look on his brow deepened. In a bare whisper he said, "James, my parents and my little brothers will be in constant danger once that ironclad is afloat."

That was the first time I had ever heard Robert express concern about his family. It was the first time he had spoken with concern about anyone but himself. Before I could say a word, he pushed back his chair and began once more to pace around the room.

After awhile he again sat down and said, "A gentleman came to the meeting. An engineer who spoke with a Swedish accent . . . a fellow named Ericsson . . ."

"Ericsson?" I repeated in disbelief. "You can't mean John Ericsson of New York City?"

Robert nodded, so I handed him the book I had been reading and said, "These are the writings and sketches of Mr. Ericsson. He has one of the keenest engineering minds of our century. In the past 30 years he has designed hundreds of marine engines and dozens of military structures."

Robert flipped through the pages of the book before tossing it onto my desk. "I hope Mr. Ericsson is as clever as you say, for he has proposed an impossible feat. He has sworn that he can build an ironclad in only 100 working days. He vowed that his ironclad will destroy the *Merrimack* or, at the very least, stop it from destroying our fleet."

Excitement traveled through my veins like quickened blood and I asked, "Did the Navy Board accept Mr. Ericsson's proposal?"

"The commodores rejected his plan at once," Robert said, "which angered Mr. Ericsson. He demanded to know the board's reason for rejecting his design and one of the commodores explained that his ship would be heavy—too heavy to have stability and thus, too heavy to float. Mr. Ericsson must be a proud man, James, because in spite of his rejection, he stayed another hour to explain the principle of buoyancy in simple terms so that all of us soon understood the reasons his ironclad would have been able to float."

Grinning, Robert said, "After Mr. Ericsson left the meeting, my father picked up a paper-board model of the ironclad and said, 'All I have to say is what the girl said when she put her foot into the stocking. It strikes me there's something in it.' My father's meaning was clear, James . . . he was instructing the Navy Board to carefully consider Mr. Ericsson's design." Robert's grin deepened as he added, "The commodores must have been as satisfied with Mr. Ericsson's explanation as my father had been. Before I had finished packing my cases to return here, it was decided that Mr. Ericsson would receive the contract to build our Union's first ironclad. And even though the contract has yet to be drawn and signed, Mr. Ericsson has since returned to New York City and has begun the construction of his ironclad."

Thinking out loud I wondered, "It is nearly impossible to build a wooden ship in 100 days. Could a ship of iron be built so quickly?"

I didn't expect a response from Robert, but he answered, "Mr. Ericsson has no choice . . . he must complete his ironclad in a few short months. Spies have informed my father that the Confederate's iron-clad will be placed in the water in three months' time. Mr. Ericsson's ironclad must destroy the *Merrimack* while she sits in dry dock—before she is placed in the water. Once the rebels launch their ironclad she could destroy our fleet at Hampton Roads—perhaps much of Washington—perhaps my family."

I didn't sleep that night. I thought only of Mr. Ericsson's promise to construct an ironclad in a few short weeks and by dawn his promise had become my new dream.

Early the next morning, I withdrew myself as a student from Harvard's Engineering School, and as afternoon waned into night, I boarded a train bound for New York City. I had one intention: to seek out Mr. Ericsson, so as to offer him my services in the construction of his iron ship.

Chapter Two

At five in the morning, my train pulled into New York City. After hiring an agent to deliver my luggage to my parents' home near Central Park, I ordered a cab.

My driver claimed he knew everyone of importance in New York City. Indeed, he knew of Mr. Ericsson and of his office in lower Manhattan and after some time he pulled up in front of a brick building with a wooden sign that bore the inventor's name.

My knock was answered by a stoop-shouldered clerk and after I had explained my purpose for being there he told me that Mr. Ericsson was away at the Continental Iron Works' ship house in Greenpoint, Long Island. It took awhile to hail another cab, but soon I was speeding towards Long Island.

Much time passed before my carriage drew up before a long flat building marked Continental Iron Works, and after I had instructed the driver to wait for me, I hurried down the pier and entered a ship house.

The building was filled with noise and dust; the noise of workers hammering and soldering sheets of iron and the dust of sawed wood and dirty floors. I walked past aproned men pouring molten iron into oddly-shaped molds and around perspiring men grouped behind vats of steaming water.

A massive desk filled one corner of the long ship house and I headed towards it, hopeful that the clerk, sitting there, could direct me to Mr. Ericsson.

Before I reached the desk I passed two men, arguing about a thick iron bar. It appeared that neither man could lift the bar, and both men blamed their inability on each other. As they argued, a giant man, crouching near the vats, stood up and strode towards them.

I am nearly six feet tall, but compared to that giant I felt like a small boy. He stood perhaps six feet, six inches and weighed several hundred pounds, but he was not given to fat for he looked like a mythical giant, muscular and strong. His shoulders were broad, his chest was expansive, and the rolled-up sleeves of his soiled shirt revealed powerful arms as thick as tree trunks. His face was that of a man of advanced age, perhaps fifty or sixty years, but he carried himself like a much younger man. In his face I saw both strength and wisdom; his strength was conveyed by his prominent nose and large, clear eyes; and his wisdom was conveyed by his wide forehead. Indeed, his forehead was so high that at first I thought him bald, but, in fact, thick hair draped his large head and grey sideburns covered his jaws and met at his chin.

He said not a word to the quarreling workers; instead, he picked up the iron bar and tossed it onto a pile of similar pieces of iron. As the giant strode back towards the vat, I overheard one of the quarrelsome workers say, "By criminy, that bar weighed 600 pounds and he lifted it like a stick of pinewood."

I looked back towards the giant worker; he was stirring the vat with a large wooden pole and amazed by his show of strength, I continued on towards the desk.

The clerk listened to my reason for being there and without making a comment he asked me to follow him. He led me back across the ship house towards the row of vats where the giant and other workers were stirring hot water. Near them stood a thinnish man in a dark suit who was measuring the temperature of the water; as he leaned over one tub, the steam fogged up his spectacles so he removed them often to wipe them with a handkerchief. I watched him with growing excitement. Often I had hoped of meeting the legendary engineer, but yet, when I was about to be introduced to him, I found myself strangely tongue-tied. I was, therefore, rather relieved that the clerk spoke for me. He said, "Excuse me, Mr. Ericsson, this young gentleman, Mr. James Hamilton, is a student of engineering at Harvard. He has taken a leave of absence from his studies to offer his services to you in the building of the ironclad."

I studied the face of the thin, bespectacled man, but his expression remained the same and unnerved by his dull reaction, I quickly extended my hand in greeting. He ignored me. Instead, the giant worker grasped my hand and shaking it hard he said, "It's a pleasure to meet you, Mr. Hamilton. We will talk in a moment and decide if you can, indeed, help me."

I was glad that Mr. Ericsson wanted to speak at a later time, for in my surprise that the giant was he, I had completely lost my voice.

Chapter Three

Another hour passed before Mr. Ericsson met me at the desk and drawing up a chair he asked me to fully explain my purpose in seeking him out. I told him what Robert Lincoln had confided and of my desire to help him fulfill his contract in any capacity he could place me. He asked me about my studies at Harvard and he seemed amused that I had read his book. After a moment of reflection about my offer of service he opened a notebook, tore off a piece of paper and scribbled down an address. Handing me the paper he said, "Go to my home and tell my wife that I will not be home for supper. If you report Mrs. Ericsson's reaction to me truthfully, I will take you on as an assistant."

I thought his condition for service strangely eccentric, but I took the cab to his home and asked the maid who answered the door to summon her mistress, Mrs. Ericsson.

How could I begin to describe the beauty of the woman who, soon, stood before me. Mrs. Ericsson was tall, as tall as myself, and large of bone like her husband though gracefully formed. Her face was sculpted with perfection; the lines of her slender nose and high cheekbones and round chin were delicately shaped. White-blonde tresses circled her ivory face, a face as unblemished and unlined as a girl of twenty though she must have been nearing thirty years. Her eyes were blue, bluer than any sky, and her lips were naturally rouged without the aid of cosmetic or paint. She spoke with a stronger Swedish accent than her husband's, so strong that at first I had difficulty understanding her.

I repeated her husband's message that he would be absent from supper that evening and at once the beauty of her face changed as her features took on a fury that is impossible to describe. Her blue eyes sparked like flicks of lightning and her lips pulled down into a frown that aged her at once. I could hear the gnash of her teeth. She clenched them so tightly together that her chin quivered and then, in an explosion of anger, she shouted at me in her own language—none of which I understood. After awhile she calmed herself and in English she said, "I have never seen you before. Do you work for my husband?"

I introduced myself and admitted that I was uncertain if Mr. Ericsson intended to accept my services before she asked, "Have you a wife or a sweetheart?"

"Neither," I answered.

She smiled bitterly and said, "Then I will tell you this, Mr. Hamilton. If you do work under my husband you will learn much for he is unequalled as an engineer and inventor. But if you should marry, do not imitate his shabby treatment of wives. Of me! Mr. Ericsson leaves me alone, night after night. He prefers to work on those blasted ships—I hate the very thought of his new ship, his new love, the ironclad. She is his only love, not me."

She nodded her head at the maid who handed me my hat and as I was leaving Mrs. Ericsson cried, "Wait! I have a message for my husband. Tell him that if he does not join me for supper by eight o'clock tonight I will pack my bags at five minutes past eight and leave him. Do you understand my message, young man?"

I nodded and bowing to her, I escaped through the door and down the walk to the cab. All the way back to the ship house I tried to decide how to relay her threatening message to Mr. Ericsson without insulting him or his wife, but in the end I repeated her message word for word. Upon hearing it, Mr. Ericsson slapped me on the shoulder, nearly knocking me down as he said, "Mr. Hamilton, I give you credit for repeating my wife's exact message. Don't look so concerned, young man. Mrs. Ericsson threatens to leave me every night and every night she is waiting for me at our door." He laughed, his laughter booming across the ship house, and added, "Mr. Hamilton, I judge you an honest man, worthy of my trust. Report here tomorrow morning at exactly 6 o'clock."

* * * * *

Dusk was falling when the cab reached my home at the edge of Central Park in New York City. At the front door a maid told me that my parents were waiting for me in the library.

I saw at once that both mother and father were displeased by my decision to leave school; my father stood stiffly before the hearth with his arms crossed and my mother's eyes were red and swollen. She smiled at me and taking my hands in hers, she kissed me on my forehead. I sat down beside her and waited for my father to speak.

He kept his back to me for a long moment and I knew from past experience that he was trying to control his temper. After some time he turned and faced me, but still said nothing as he lit his cigar; his hands shook slightly and I realized with some surprise that I had never seen him so angry. Finally, he spoke in a voice that was flat and low. He said, "James, your mother and I are deeply disturbed by your rash decision to leave Harvard. Deeply disturbed. Whatever possessed you to leave school at the beginning of the term?"

My mother averted her face from me, but not before I noticed the tears that glazed her gentle eyes. I regretted the misunderstanding I had caused—the note I had sent with my luggage must have confused them, for it had only mentioned my arrival in New York and my withdrawal from college. And so I told them Robert Lincoln's news about the *Merrimack* and of Mr. Ericsson's contract to build an ironclad in 100 days. I told them, too, of my decision to seek him out and assist him in his work. I emphasized the danger the *Merrimack* posed to our federal fleet, to Washington and perhaps to Mr. Lincoln, himself (my father is a staunch Republican so I hoped to appease some of his anger by stressing the danger to our President). My father listened to all I said without interruption before he said, "Your decision to withdraw from school before you were certain that Mr. Ericsson would accept you was premature. James, all your life you have acted impulsively, rashly. Still, your intention to serve our country is admirable."

My mother cradled my hand in hers and smiling she said, "I am proud of you, James."

"We are both proud of you, son," my father interjected, "even though your mother and I had hoped you would remain at Harvard until your graduation."

I assured my parents that I would return to Harvard upon the completion of Mr. Ericsson's ironclad. Father's face brightened with relief, and mother embraced me even as her eyes misted with fresh tears. Supper, later that evening, was filled with excited discussion about the war, in general, and ironclads, in particular, but I retired early and left my parents to their coffee. I needed sleep. Before dawn broke, I was astride my horse, galloping towards Long Island.

Chapter Four

In September . . .

I studied Mr. Ericsson's design of the ironclad: the two hulls, the engines, the revolving turrets, the deck, the magazines and the staterooms.

Once completed, the bottom, or lower hull, would measure a full six feet in depth. That hull would be flattened on the bottom with slanted sides and would be submerged under water at all times. It would house the engines, the boilers (that produce the steam for power), the magazines (storage for the ammunition), the staterooms (quarters for the crew and officers); and a mechanism that would turn the turret (gun tower). The entire hull would be covered with iron, one-half inch thick.

The upper hull would fit over the bottom hull. And yet, though the upper hull would only measure five feet deep, it would be longer and wider than the bottom hull. The upper hull would be exposed to enemy fire, so the vertical sides of the hull would be covered with heavy iron plates; plates that would be strong enough to keep cannonballs from crashing through the ship's sides.

The deck of the ironclad would have two layers: a bottom layer of wood and an upper layer of iron, one-inch thick. What interested me the most about the design of the deck was its center area where a wide, brass ring (20 feet in diameter) would be placed. For that space, Mr. Ericsson designed a turret, a cylinder twenty feet wide and nine feet high, that would have openings for two guns. Those guns, heavy caliber Dahlgren guns, would be placed side by side. The genius of Mr. Ericsson's turret was that the tower would be able to revolve in any direction, so regardless of the ship's position in the water, the guns could be pointed at any target. The turning of the turret would be possible because of Mr. Ericsson's unique design for gears and an engine that he labelled a "donkey" engine.

Because of the short length of time to complete the job, Mr. Ericsson assigned contracts to several companies. The hulls were being built by the Rowland Ironworks Company in the same ship house that Mr. Ericsson spent much of his time. The armor plates were being made in Baltimore, Maryland, and delivered to New York, by the fastest possible route. The engine had been entrusted to master engineers at the Delameter Company, and the turret was being made by a company called Novelty Iron Works.

Mr. Ericsson spent all day and most of the hours of night at his drafting board sketching designs. When completed there would be 3,000 separate parts of the ship. On most days I was asked to take his finished designs, re-check the measurements against his original plans, and then enter those measurements into a journal he was keeping for the Navy Department. Then, if necessary, I assigned messengers to deliver his designs to the craftsmen who would trace or mold each part in wood or iron.

* * * * *

In October . . .

I was in the office when a package from the Navy Board was delivered by courier. Mr. Ericsson opened the envelope and read for a full minute before his face colored a purplish-red hue and he exploded into his native language. Somehow I knew he was cursing in Swedish, though I understood none of what he said.

Just as his wife had, when she, too, had exploded into Swedish, he soon calmed himself and in English said to me, "James, years ago I swore I would never deal with the navy, and here I am again, working without rest and reward and today I receive their contract. I have a good mind not to sign it. According to this contract, I am obligated to refund the government for all materials and labor if my ironclad fails to do three things . . ." He slammed his fist down on the table and shouted, "One, the gun tower must revolve while firing as promised; two, the ironclad must reach a speed of nine miles an hour; and three, the ironclad must remain buoyant—it must float as promised! The navy distrusts my design! Those commodores, those fools, have insulted me for the final time!"

He again lapsed into a flurry of Swedish and then of a sudden he said, "I have no choice, James. I must sign or my financial backers will lose the money they have already invested and, after all, they are not merely my partners . . . they are my good friends." He snatched up a pen, signed his name and added, "But I swear I will never work with the navy again."

I smiled to myself because I knew that no matter how much he complained about the Navy Department, Mr. Ericsson would cooperate as long as his designs were needed.

On the twenty-fifth of October the keel of the ironclad was laid. I decided that day that I would follow

Mr. Ericsson's example. Like him, I wanted to devote my entire life to building our nation's fleet into the greatest navy the world will ever witness.

* * * * *

In November . . .

I read in the New York newspapers that Mr. Ericsson's ironclad had been labelled "Ericsson's Folly." Bets of money, both large and small sums, were being placed by ordinary citizens who wagered that his ship of iron would sink the moment it was launched. Mr. Ericsson never read those critical stories, for he never took the time to read a newspaper. Indeed, he never took time for anything else but his work. Day after day and much of every night he bent over his draft board drawing and changing his designs for the ironclad.

Mr. Ericsson never asked me to deliver another message to his wife. There was no need to, as she followed through with her threat to leave him. At the beginning of October she sailed to Europe on one of her husband's own ships. There were rumors that she had rented a townhouse in London, England, and that she stubbornly refused to return until her husband promised to limit his working hours. Mr. Ericsson never spoke about his wife, but he wrote her daily letters which I posted for him along with his business correspondence.

After his wife's departure, there was a quietness about Mr. Ericsson as though some of his lifeblood had drained away. His working hours grew longer and I suspected that he dreaded going home to his empty house. It seemed ages ago that he had asked me to deliver his message to his wife, but I will always remember her words of advice and warning: her advice to learn what I could from her genius

husband and her warning to avoid his only flaw—
his habit of working long hours. If I should ever
marry, I would not neglect my wife; I wouldn't want
to experience Mr. Ericsson's loneliness, for it surrounded him like a cold shadow.

* * * * *

In December . . .

I was given an opportunity to be present while
the engines were fitted. By then I had memorized
Mr. Ericsson's design and I swear, if given the proper
materials and time, I could have constructed the engine myself. None of which I would have learned at
Harvard, but I intended to keep my promise to my
parents and return there in a few months. Until then
I was content to stand behind Mr. Ericsson's shoulder and learn the skills a student engineer can only
learn from a master engineer such as himself.

One such engineering skill I acquired was the
necessity of knowing your design so thoroughly that
modifications could be made without delay. I learned
that skill by watching Mr. Ericsson. On occasion, over
the past several months, craftsmen appeared at his
desk with complaints that a particular part didn't fit
into another part, and I'd watch as Mr. Ericsson took
white chalk and without hesitation marked modi-
fied designs directly on those pieces of iron or wood.
I understood, then, that every one of the 3,000 parts
of Mr. Ericsson's design was firmly implanted in his
memory. It was as though his ship was a giant jig-
saw puzzle and Mr. Ericsson could pick up one piece
and know exactly where it would fit in the overall
picture of his ship's design.

Throughout the holiday season my mother
seemed determined to introduce me to every maiden
she met, but there was no time for suppers or con-
certs for the ironclad was being prepared for an
important day, December 30. On that day Mr. Ericsson

applied steam to the ironclad's engines for the first time.

* * * * *

In January . . .

I was included in the small group of workmen and assistants who joined Mr. Ericsson on the deck of the ironclad. A constant rain, light though icy, misted the air, but none of us minded the chill of the morning for we were about to witness a grand moment of history—the launching of the Union's first ironclad.

Mr. Ericsson stood in the center of our group; his powerful arms were crossed over his chest; and his face was turned upwards. I thought he was studying the overcast sky, but someone whispered, "Mr. Ericsson is praying." I believe, then, that we all began to pray. My own prayers, however, were disturbed by the sight of the hundreds of people who had gathered on the docks; many of whom had placed money bets that the ironclad would sink to the ocean floor. Mr. Ericsson angrily dismissed their predictions that his ship would sink, but as a precaution he had arranged a small boat to stand by.

After a while, Mr. Ericsson turned his face towards us and said, "The navy suggested that I propose a name for this floating battery. It is my opinion that this ironclad intruder will prove a severe Monitor to the leaders of the Southern Rebellion and to the European countries who wish to aid the rebels. So I will propose naming this new battery, the U.S.S. *Monitor*, for she will keep watch over our enemies."

At 10 o'clock, exactly, Mr. Ericsson removed his hat and waved it at the workers manning the braces; at once they knocked away the braces, and the ironclad slipped into the water with a loud splash.

We stood, our feet planted firmly on the wet deck, as the *Monitor* cut through the water and slid as gracefully as a sea porpoise through the cold, grey waters. Behind us, the people on the dock erupted with applause; men waved rain-soaked hats, women twirled umbrellas and children clapped mittened hands. I looked over at Mr. Ericsson; his face was a study of contrasts. He looked relieved that his ironclad had not sunk, and yet he revealed no surprise that his ship floated smoothly through the waters. And though he appeared ecstatic about his success, he also looked sad, and I wondered if he was asking himself if his ruined marriage was worth a ship of iron.

Chapter Five

On the tenth day of February, my eighteenth birthday, I was assigned the task of sketching the *Monitor*'s guns and supporting platforms. The task took a full week, but my attention to the smallest detail produced sketches that Mr. Ericsson approved of with much praise. His commendation of my work pleased me greatly, for my esteem of Mr. Ericsson is inestimable. My respect for him as an engineer and a gentleman knows no bounds.

As the month of February neared its end, Mr. Ericsson summoned me into his office and closed the door. Asking me to sit down, he took his own chair and with a frown furrowing his forehead he said, "James, last month before the launch of the *Monitor* I received a letter from Washington. It appears that the Navy Board still harbors doubts that the two guns of the *Monitor* will have an impact against the many guns of the *Merrimack*. You know my design as well as I do and your mind is quick. I want you to meet with President Lincoln and the Secretary of the Navy, Mr. Welles. Answer any

questions that plague them and give them this."
He handed me a tin box; it contained a model of
the U.S.S. *Monitor* cast from iron and wood. The
model was an exact duplicate of Mr. Ericsson's
ironclad; even the turret revolved just as the ac-
tual one will turn whence the guns are firing.

I stood up and offering Mr. Ericsson my hand I
said, "You honor me, sir, by asking me to meet with
the president in your place."

A smile touched the corners of Mr. Ericsson's
eyes. In a low voice, a voice that could barely be
heard, he said, "My wife and I were never blessed
by children . . . often I dreamt of a son following in
my path . . . a son, much like yourself, James."

There was no need for me to respond to his high
compliment, for he knew of my great respect for him.
We parted then; he was late for a meeting with his
financial backers and I had to hurry home to pack a
bag for the journey to our nation's capital.

Chapter Six

As my train approached Washington, D.C., I remembered a visit there almost three years ago. I remembered a quiet city with an almost ghost-like appearance caused by the skeletal structures of unfinished buildings and partially-built monuments. I remembered the muddied, pitted streets and the disease-ridden marshes of the surrounding swamps. And I remembered the smells of the city, the stink of the scum-covered Potomac River and the salts of the marshland and the stench of the pigs that ran wild.

Outside the train station, I hired a cab and as I rode towards Pennsylvania Avenue, it seemed that the city I remembered had been replaced by a much different city. Although the streets were still muddied, the buildings were still unfinished and the smells were still pungent, Washington had changed from a quiet city into a city touched by war.

The soiled streets were crowded with military traffic: soldiers and sailors afoot, officers on horses, army wagons pulled by teams of six horses; and cannons hauled by mules. On both sides of the streets soldiers lounged in front of private homes and shops or camped outside buildings marked as military hospitals or boardinghouses.

My carriage turned onto Pennsylvania Avenue; ahead of me, behind an iron fence, stood the Executive Mansion. I paid the cabbie and taking my bag I walked through the gate.

The door of the Executive Mansion was propped open. I didn't knock or ring a bell because other visitors, such as myself, entered freely. So, I followed a gentleman with a gold cane through the wide foyer and soon found myself in a reception room near a grand staircase.

The reception room was large; wide windows with drawn curtains allowed the sun to flood the room with light. Wooden chairs were placed against the walls; the chairs, except for a few at the far end of the room, were all taken by ladies and gentlemen. Each guest waited, I presumed, to speak to President Lincoln.

As the hours passed, individual names were called out and I watched as soldiers in soiled uniforms, ladies in crinoline gowns and business men in black suits hurried from the room, one by one, for their interviews with the president. After awhile there were only three of us waiting: myself and two ladies.

One lady, a tiny woman wizened with age, sat on a chair to my left. A web of wrinkles crisscrossed her narrow forehead, sunken cheeks and thin neck. Her eyes, when open, were small and dark, nearly as dark as her skin while the bit of hair that straggled from under her bonnet was white. She wore a tattered shawl around her shoulders and a dress that was too thin for February's weather, but in spite of her age and poverty, she was immaculate, except for the hem of her skirt that was as muddied as her boots.

The old woman's crooked posture revealed her fatigue. She was bent forward; both hands rested on the knob of her cane of twisted rosewood. Often, throughout those hours, I heard soft breathing as she dozed and woke, dozed and woke. Once, when she noticed me looking her way, she nodded at me and I saw keen intelligence in her brown eyes before they closed again in sleep.

The other lady in the room sat to my right and it was she whom I directed most of my attention toward. I will admit freely that she was the most beautiful maiden I had ever seen. She sat throughout those hours in quiet, her eyes fixed straight ahead or dropped to the book on her lap. She sat so quietly, in fact, that she might have resembled a marble statue of some ancient goddess of Rome or Greece, except for the vividness of the colors that surrounded her—the rose-colored silk of her gown, the rich colors of her hair and eyes and lips. No, she could never be mistaken for a statue of cold, white marble.

I doubt she was my age; perhaps she was only seventeen or sixteen years. There was, about her, the innocence of one who had not yet realized the harsher side of life.

She sat in a chair under a tall window and as the hours passed and the sun changed its position in the sky, the sunlight that touched her hair changed its very color. Her hair was the color of mahogany wood, a brown enriched with dark red, but under the changing light her hair took on colors of gold and bronze and fire. I found myself as fascinated by the ever-changing colors of her hair as a boy watching colors change through a kaleidoscope.

The bright sun was not content to merely change the color of her hair. Under its light her skin, as white as alabaster, took on an almost transparent hue, and her eyes took on the color of navy, much like the navy-blue waters of an ocean at night.

She looked my way once or twice, but her attention stayed focused on a small notebook that she wrote in from time to time. I sat in silent frustration, trying to think of some way to address her besides the usual polite greeting, but I could think of nothing clever to say.

A servant appeared in the doorway and called out the name "Miss Betsy" and the elderly Negress stirred from her sleep. I stood up with the intention of offering her assistance, but she leapt from her chair and walked rapidly through the door.

Still on my feet I glanced over at the maiden, but she was absorbed in her book so I took a different chair, a chair placed closer to hers. Clearing my throat I said, "I hope our interviews can be worked into Mr. Lincoln's schedule today."

She looked up at me and closing the book she smiled her reply, "One can only hope so."

Her smile was radiant; her smile lent a luminous quality to her eyes; her smile caused my heart to pound uncontrollably. She opened her notebook and began again to write. My mind went blank as I struggled to find something sensible to comment on and in desperation I asked, "Are you an author?"

She looked at me with a puzzled expression and then glancing down at her notebook she laughed, "Heavens no, I am not a writer, nor would I ever want to be, for I can't think of a more boring profession." She handed me the notebook and I read the cover, "Sanitation Fair."

She explained, "I have been writing down my suggestions for Washington's Sanitation Fair that will be conducted this spring. Our goal is to raise two thousand dollars to purchase cloth, needles and thread. Our soldiers and sailors are in dire need of better uniforms."

"Very commendable," I said. "Are you here to bring your work to the attention of Mr. Lincoln?"

She smiled and said, "My interview is not with our president. I am waiting for his wife, Mrs. Lincoln, for she is a member of our committee." She paused a moment and then added, "I'm sorry, sir, but I can't quite place your name."

I apologized for my rudeness and introduced myself at once. Her name, I learned, was Miss Julia Holmes, a name that sounded familiar. "Years ago," I told her, "my family visited here from New York— during our stay my parents introduced me to an old friend of theirs, Judge Oliver Holmes."

"My father," she answered softly. An expression of pain shadowed her luminous eyes and she looked down at her book, but I was determined to keep her navy-blue eyes turned towards me. Clearing my throat I began again by saying, "I will be staying overnight before my return to New York. Could you recommend decent lodging?"

"The Willard," she answered at once and then before I could ask her to dine with me, the servant appeared at the door and announced my name. I stood and bowed to Miss Holmes and with reluctance I left her sitting alone.

Chapter Seven

I was ushered into a small room where the Secretary of Navy, Mr. Gideon Welles, was seated at a round table; beside him sat Miss Betsy, the elderly Negro woman. She sat like a wood carving, unmoving except for her clever, brown eyes that watched me through narrowed slits. In front of her, on the table, lay the twisted rosewood cane.

Mr. Welles was a robust fellow with a thick beard that covered much of his face. In a calm voice, almost too low to be heard, he said, "I must apologize for President Lincoln . . . he has been called away on an emergency, so I must conduct this interview for him." He then introduced the Negress and himself before saying, "Miss Betsy has just given me an account of her past week. In my opinion, it is a story that you, too, should hear firsthand."

Miss Betsy turned her wary eyes on me and in a voice far too strong for her tiny size she said, "I cook for the rebels at the Navy Yard in Norfolk. A man I knows there is a mechanic. He drawed a picture of the rebel's iron ship. He asked me to give his picture to Mr. Welles—said I can find him here in Father Abraham's house."

She rubbed a hand across her wrinkled cheek and said, "My grandson drives a hay cart from Norfolk to rebel camps in Virginny. One morning he hides me under the hay. That wagon near shakes my teeth out . . . we rides all day into the night . . . in the dark time my grandson drops me in some woods. I start walking here to this city. I walk two, three, four days . . . one day I walks near a rebel's camp—rebels call me old cripple Negress—theys throw sharp stones at me. But I don't look their way. Keeps on walking and eating berries off the bushes and drinking cooling water from the rivers. I never stops walking—if the rebels find the picture they whip me or shoot me dead—rebels don't take kindly to spies—theys kill Negro spies. Nearing day I comes to this grand city . . . takes all morning to find Father Abraham's house."

To my continued astonishment, Mr. Welles picked up her cane, twisted off the top knob and pulled a piece of paper from the hollowed out tube. Handing it to me I smoothed out the paper and read:

> The C.S.S. Virginia (the former U.S.S. Merrimack) has been taken out of dry dock. The Confederates are finishing her armaments. She will be battle ready by March 1.

I looked over at Mr. Welles as he said, "The government's original contract with Mr. Ericsson called for him to destroy the *Merrimack* while she was still in dry dock. Now that the rebels' ironclad is afloat, armed and dangerous, the *Monitor* must battle her on water. My question to you, Mr. Hamilton, is a simple one . . . can the *Monitor* with only two guns destroy the *Merrimack* with her ten guns?"

Before answering, I opened the tin box and took out the model of the *Monitor*. Placing it in the middle

Drawing by Joy Renee Maine

of the table I explained, "The *Merrimack* may have eight more guns, but she must position herself in the water to fire in the direction that is needed." Using my finger I turned the turret of the model and said, "On the other hand, the *Monitor*'s turret revolves, and therefore she can take any position in the water and still fire at her target. Thus the *Monitor*, though smaller and armed with only two guns, is a far more dangerous ironclad than the *Merrimack*."

A long silence met my explanation so I continued, "The sketch that Miss Betsy has so bravely provided points out the *Merrimack*'s most obvious weakness: her large size. Be assured that her movement in the water will be awkward and slow of speed. Mr. Ericsson has already determined a second weakness: the *Merrimack*'s engine, an engine that was once condemned, will prove untrustworthy in the heat of battle. On the other hand, Mr. Ericsson's *Monitor* is small and only a small portion of the ship will be above water, so she will offer a minute target for the *Merrimack*'s guns. And because of her smaller size and her powerful engines the *Monitor* will move swiftly through the water."

Mr. Welles picked up the model and turning it in his hands, he examined it from every angle before passing it to Miss Betsy. Then he asked, "When do you return to New York?"

"On the morning train, Mr. Secretary," I answered.

He rolled up the sketch of the *Merrimack*, handed it to me and said, "Take this to Mr. Ericsson. No doubt it will inspire him to complete his work on the *Monitor*. Be sure to stress that the navy can only give him a few hours' notice when his ship is needed for battle. And remind him, Mr. Hamilton, that the very existence of our nation may depend on the *Monitor*'s destruction of the *Merrimack*."

Chapter Eight

I returned at once to the reception room, but Miss Holmes was gone. Disappointed, I spent the next hour roaming about the streets of Washington. As I walked, my thoughts troubled me—troubling thoughts of the *Merrimack*, already afloat and dangerous, and equally troubling thoughts of the beautiful maiden who had disappeared from my life like a wind-blown cloud. After some time, I came by accident across the Willard, the hotel that Miss Holmes had recommended. I left my bag with the front desk and after questioning a clerk who claimed he knew everyone in the city, I learned Miss Holmes' address.

I hired a carriage and soon drew up in front of a brick house encircled by a high fence. The iron gate was unlatched; taking a deep breath I walked up the curving path towards the porch.

Miss Holmes, I was told, was not at home, but the grey-haired maid, who answered the door, invited me into the parlor. For the next two hours I sat on an overstuffed chair and listened to the ticking of a clock.

The grandfather clock was chiming the hour of five when I heard the front door open. I sat up straighter hoping the light footsteps in the hall belonged to Miss Holmes, but at the same time wondering if I had made a mistake in presuming she would be pleased to see me again. Perhaps she was betrothed . . .

When she came into the parlor, the expression on her face told me that I hadn't made a mistake. Rising to my feet I bowed and said, "Miss Holmes, forgive my rash behavior. I know we are practically strangers, but would you do me the honor of dining with me this evening?"

She smiled, "I would gladly accept your kind invitation, Mr. Hamilton, but on one condition . . . that you use my given name, Julia."

I asked her, in turn, to call me James and she repeated my name twice as though trying to fit it to my face.

* * * * *

When we walked into the dining room at the Willard, gentlemen young and old, looked our way; no wonder, for Julia's beauty brightened the darkened room like a star in the night.

We were seated at a corner table, lit by a small candle; near us, beside a fountain of goldfish, stood a violinist playing softly. Around us sat other diners, but I saw no other face nor heard no other voice, but Julia's. Julia . . . the sound of her name floated around me like the sounds of the violin.

The candlelight on Julia's hair reminded me of the way the sun had changed the colors of her hair. I wanted to touch her hair, kiss her hair, but instead I said, "Julia, you have asked me about my studies, my family and my work under Mr. Ericsson, but you have told me nothing of yourself."

Joy Renee Maine

She seemed surprised by my curiosity, for she asked, "What is it you wish to know about me, James?"

"Everything," I answered.

She laughed and picking up her goblet of water, she sipped it before saying, "Perhaps I should first tell you of my afternoon. My meeting with Mrs. Lincoln was pleasant. Despite what the newspapers report, she is a charming lady and in complete support of the Sanitary Commission. Mrs. Lincoln has suggested an art auction to raise the money, for there are several painters and sculptors living in Washington who would surely contribute a few pieces."

I was determined to learn if Julia had a beau and so I asked in a casual tone, "I suppose you have become acquainted with many gentleman and military officers through your work with the commission?"

Smiling, she answered playfully, "I only acquaint myself with gentlemen, whether they are civilians or military men. I prefer not to speak to rogues." She smiled again and said, "The answer to your question, James, is no. I have met few gentlemen through my work with the commission. I have met many military men, however, through my involvement in this war."

"Your involvement in this war?" I repeated.

She again picked up her water goblet, but she hesitated as though she had forgotten to drink and looking beyond me, somewhere into her past, she said, "Last summer, I was one of the picnickers who witnessed the Battle of Bull Run. My escort, a cowardly man, deserted me during the riot and I was rescued by a sergeant, a kindly gentleman named Sergeant Nathan Taylor. During our ride back to Washington, I ministered to the wounded soldiers he carried in his wagon. One of those soldiers was my sister's own fiancée, Major Adam Sorenson . . . Adam was grievously injured at Bull Run and there was nothing more I could do for him except bind up his wounds and offer him water . . . you can not imagine how terrible it was to watch Adam and the others suffer during that long ride back to Washington. It was during those hours that I vowed to involve my-self in this war."

"When we first met," I admitted to her, "I thought you looked far too young, too . . . protected to have seen the harsher side of life . . . I was wrong."

She said, "Until that day at Bull Run I did lead a protected life. Until then I deliberately ignored life's . . . harsher side. In one short day the war aged me, the war wrought changes in me. Changes for the better."

I pressed her to explain her meaning and she said, "Before that picnic . . . before the Battle at Bull Run . . . and before my ministry to the wounded, I believed that the entire world danced around me. Only me. I was a selfish, spoiled girl. James, if we had met a year ago before Bull Run, I seriously doubt that you would have found your way to my home and I doubt we would be dining together this evening."

She laughed at my protest and said, "Believe me, James, I was terribly spoiled." Her laughter faded and though she still smiled, her smile was traced with sadness. "James, when we first spoke today you mentioned my father. Where and when did you meet him?"

I hesitated, trying to remember clearly before saying, "It was three years ago. In April. My parents and I were in the garden of the Smithsonian Institute when we came across your father. I remember that he was walking with a woman, a rather beautiful woman."

"My mother," Julia said in a soft voice. "Every afternoon, if the weather was fair, my father left the courthouse and met my mother there. She loved the gardens of the institute . . . especially the roses that wound along the paths. It was a place that she never tired of visiting and father never tired of meeting her there, for he cherished her so."

In spite of the dim lamps I could see that Julia's eyes were misting when she said, "Two summers ago my father had to travel to Virginia on court business. At the last moment he convinced my mother to travel with him . . . their train derailed on the side of a mountain . . . everyone, including my parents, plunged to their deaths. I should have told you at once, when you first mentioned my father, but at times I cannot bear to speak of their deaths."

"How old were you at that time?" I asked.

"I was fourteen. My sister, Louisa, had just celebrated her sixteenth birthday, but she was named my guardian . . . she'll remain my guardian until my eighteenth birthday. I am now sixteen years."

Julia looked at the flickering candle and then at me again before saying, "Thank you, James, for asking about my parents. You reminded me of their walks in the garden. You brought back another memory of their love for each other." She looked long into my face as though she was studying me and then she blushed and said, "Forgive me, I was staring at you . . . at your eyes . . . your eyes are the exact color of amber wood . . . father gave my mother a brooch of brown amber on their wedding day." Her blush deepened and she said, "Perhaps you find my words rather forward."

"Not at all," I assured her.

Her cheeks were nearly crimson with embarrassment as she explained, "I have always been fascinated by eyes. My father was fond of saying that the eyes are the windows to your soul and I think there is much wisdom in that sentiment. Adam . . . Louisa's betrothed . . . had eyes of green emerald . . . his clear green eyes revealed the goodness of his soul. A few hours before he died . . . he was too weak to speak . . . his eyes spoke instead of his passionate love for my sister."

My heart pounded like a drum. I asked, my voice low, "What do my eyes reveal about me?"

"Your eyes reveal that you are a dreamer. Whilst you were speaking about your desire to build ships, your eyes warmed with the wonder of your desire . . . I think, perhaps, that you dream of ships . . ."

She was interrupted by our waiter and while we ate, we spoke about everything until the candle burned to its wick.

*　*　*　*　*

Although we had spoken for hours at the Willard, we drove through the streets of Washington in silence as though both of us had thoughts to ponder. My thoughts were of Julia and the dismal fact that I would have to leave her on the morrow. What her thoughts were, I didn't know, but a smile lingered in her eyes. In the near distance, a church bell chimed the midnight hour as our carriage pulled up before her home. Neither of us spoke, neither of us wanted to speak words of farewell. I lifted her down from the carriage, and offering my arm we passed through her gate.

Julia paused just beyond the fence, under a wooden trellis that arched over the cobblestone path. The sky above us was studded with stars, large, white stars that threw down their light. Julia looked up at me, her eyes shimmering as though they had robbed the stars of their very light, and said, "My mother so loved roses that she planted a rose bush on either side of this trellis . . . there, she placed a red rose bush for my father and there, she planted a white rose bush for herself. Over the years, since my parents' death, the roses have climbed up over the trellis . . . during the summer months, red and white roses create a canopy of flowers atop the trellis." She gazed up as though picturing the blossoms that would soon bloom there and said, "My sister, Louisa, and I love to stand beneath this trellis. It was here, under the canopy of roses, that Adam proposed to Louisa. And it was here that Louisa watched for Adam's face amongst the thousands of soldiers marching off to Bull Run . . . Louisa waited here for hours just to bid him goodbye." Julia smiled at me; under the stars' soft light her eyes glistened with tears. She asked, "Must you leave Washington so soon, James? I fear we shall never meet again."

I took her hands and said, "I have no choice in the matter, Julia. I must deliver important information to Mr. Ericsson. When the train leaves at dawn, I must be on it."

"Then," she whispered, "farewell," and pulling away from me she rushed up the path towards her door.

Chapter Nine

The morning sky was graying as the sun pushed its way through a strand of clouds. I stood on the platform, searching for Julia's face, but there were only passengers, such as myself, waiting for the train. Slowly, I walked up and down the platform, staring into carriages that rolled by, hoping against hope that she might come to see me off, but as the train pulled into the station I lost all hope.

As I stepped up on the train, I heard someone call out, "James . . ." and jerking around I saw Julia running across the platform, her shawl falling from her shoulders.

The conductor waved his lantern to signal the train's departure, but I leapt to the platform and ran to meet her. We clutched each other's hands, without speaking, for we were content to merely look at each other. It was then that I noticed the brooch pinned to her collar, an oval brooch of brown amber.

I asked, "Julia, is that your mother's wedding brooch?"

She smiled and murmured, "Yes, I shall wear it until we meet again, James. Mother's brooch will remind me of your amber eyes. Your dreamer eyes."

A shrill whistle blew a final warning as the train slowly moved forward. I had to be on that train; in my pocket was the sketch of the *Merrimack*. I held Julia's hands tightly and though I knew I shouldn't, I kissed her mouth. Our one kiss avowed our love for each other.

The train was gaining speed; I grabbed my bag and running down the platform I jumped towards the steps of the caboose. Then, looking back, I saw Julia standing alone, her hand touching the brooch at her throat.

Joy Renee Maine

Chapter Ten

A short while after the *Monitor* was berthed in the deep harbor of the Brooklyn Navy Yard, my father suggested that I return the books I had borrowed from Mr. Ericsson. That was father's subtle reminder that I keep my promise to return to Harvard.

Mr. Ericsson was in his office making final notes about the *Monitor*'s turret. Just as I placed the books on the corner of his desk a government courier appeared at the door with a sealed envelope. Curious, I watched Mr. Ericsson's face change as he read the enclosed message before jotting down a brief reply and handing it back to the courier.

Even before the door had closed behind the messenger, Mr. Ericsson exploded in an excited voice, "James, the federal army under General McClellan is moving up the Yorktown peninsula towards Richmond. If the general is successful, the war could end in a matter of weeks."

Mr. Ericcson stood up abruptly as though his excitement had pushed him to his feet. He said, "The *Monitor* has been ordered to Hampton Roads as a precautionary measure. As yet, the *Merrimack* has not made her appearance on the water, but the rebels may use her to attack the boats transporting General McClellan's soldiers. If the *Merrimack* does appear, the *Monitor* must destroy her."

All at once, Mr. Ericsson grew silent; a silence I had come to recognize as a sign that he was considering something important. I waited, my own excitement growing, and at last he said, "James, I assumed I would have been allowed to accompany the crew of the ironclad so as to make observations, but I had assumed wrong. The navy worries that I might consider myself the ironclad's other commodore; however, permission was granted for one of my assistants to take my place aboard ship. I have considered the navy's offer carefully. The man I selected would have to be responsible enough to record accurate observations about every part of the ship: the turret, the guns, the engine, the ventilation system—every blasted part. I have chosen you, James, to serve as my eyes and ears aboard the *Monitor*."

My blood pounded in my veins. Stumbling over my words I thanked him saying, "Sir, I consider it a privilege and an honor to serve in your place."

Mr. Ericsson smiled broadly and shaking my hand he said, "Keep in mind, James, that you will be a civilian aboard a naval ship. Take careful, detailed notes, but do not interfere with the crew's duties, unless you are needed."

* * * * *

There were only a few hours before the *Monitor*'s departure at noon, but I had to return home to break the news to my parents.

I found mother in the conservatory, clipping leaves off a miniature fig tree. As always, upon greeting me, she took my hands in hers before kissing my forehead, but this time she paused and staring into my eyes she gasped, "James, what's wrong?"

I wondered what she had seen in my expression. Excitement about the coming voyage? Fear about a possible battle? Sadness that I might never see her and my father again? I forced myself to smile to ease her worries and said, "Mr. Ericsson has asked me to observe aboard the *Monitor*. We leave for Virginia in a few hours."

My mother studied my face, reading my thoughts and hearing the words I had left unspoken. In a trembling voice she asked, "Is this something you feel you must do, James?"

I nodded.

"Have you told your father, yet?" she asked.

"Not yet," I replied.

"Then," she murmured sorrowfully, "we shall tell him together."

* * * * *

I packed lightly: a razor, a clean shirt, and at my father's insistence, a pistol and package of cartridges. Then, while mother ordered her carriage to the front gate, I took father aside and asked him to keep her from accompanying me to the Navy Yard. I knew if she saw me board the oddly-shaped craft that her fears would multiply, for she believed what the newspapers had reported about the *Monitor*—that the ship would prove unseaworthy. Mother had convinced herself that the *Monitor* was doomed to sink. Father agreed that she should be spared the ordeal of seeing me off, and so, I bid my parents farewell at our door. As my carriage pulled away I took care not to look back, for mother's weeping disturbed me.

* * * * *

The tugboat, *Seth Low*, attached her lines to the *Monitor* and at twelve noon, on that sixth day of March, we sailed from the Navy Yard in Brooklyn, New York, towards the open sea. The waters were calm and the skies were clear and except for the excitement churning in my stomach I expected an easy passage.

* * * * *

An hour after our departure I had finished walking through every part of the ship. It was an almost eerie walk. Each section and all the corridors were lit by small lanterns that cast off dim light. Shadows hung so deeply that sailors, walking past, appeared like ghosts out of the darkness; silent ghosts, for few spoke as if silence was mandated to retain the unearthly quiet under the sea.

I found an empty spot and opened the black notebook that Mr. Ericsson had given me; it was similar to the notebook that Julia had been writing in when we first met.

Julia. I had written to her every day since leaving Washington and she had sent daily letters to me. How was it possible that our brief time together had led us into love?

I opened the notebook and wrote:

A record of the Ironclad, the U.S.S. Monitor, *as kept by James Hamilton.*

Turning to the second page I wrote:

March 6, 1862: Departure from the Brooklyn Navy Yard as scheduled at noon. We are securely connected by wire cables to the tugboat, the Seth Low, *under Master . . .*

I wrote nothing more, for Julia captured my every thought. I turned to the back of the notebook and on the last page I wrote:

My Dearest Julia,   *March 6, 1862*

I write this letter while sailing from New York to Virginia on the U.S.S. Monitor. At some point in time this ship will pass Washington—then, the short distance between us will cause me unbearable pain, for we will not be able to meet.

Julia, upon my return to New York I must honor my parents' wishes and return to Harvard to finish my studies of engineering. After one more term I will be graduated, and then, dearest love, marry me. I would be able to provide for your every need and I would cherish you, just as your father once cherished your mother. Write to me, Julia, and fulfill my dream.

Love, eternally,

James

I tore out the page and borrowing an envelope from an engineer, I addressed and sealed the letter, before placing it in my jacket pocket. I promised myself that if I survived the voyage, I would mail the letter the moment we docked in New York.

Chapter Eleven

The first day of sailing was uneventful; the waters remained smooth and calm, so I only wrote occasional notes during those beginning hours of our voyage.

Overnight we moved from calm waters into rough seas and throughout the early morning hours the ship's jerking, rolling movement made me nauseous. By midmorning I became violently ill, and spent much time vomiting in the water closet (Mr. Ericsson's system of water-filled pipes to remove our waste products was ingenious, but, the water closet had to be used carefully. One sailor misjudged the pressure in the water and he was caught in the rush of water and thrown six feet up into the air). Before noon I had dry heaves and afterwards I laid on my cot until my stomach pains ended and I could resume my note taking.

At twelve noon, while the cook passed around rations of dry crackers, winds from the northwest began to blow. At first, the ship continued plying through the waters without too much difficulty, but as the winds increased in strength, high waves slapped against the pilothouse. Wave after wave struck the pilothouse and eventually water seeped through the small eye-slits cut in its four walls. The slits were less than an inch wide, but they circled nearly the entire width of the the pilothouse. Water shot through those narrow openings with such force that Carl, the helmsman, was knocked to the floor, but he stood back up, wiped the seawater from his face and took his place again behind the steering wheel.

Moments later, more water shot through the eye-slits and pushed Carl backwards. Again and again he stood, but water kept rushing in with incredible force. One wave hit Carl especially hard and slipping, he rammed his face against the wheel; his nose bled profusely but he hung onto the wheel with white-knuckled fists.

A sailor shouted out an alarm from the stern of the ship: the hull was filling with water. Minutes later, the second in command, Lieutenant S. Dana Greene, reported to the pilothouse that seawater had poured like a waterfall down the tower to flood the bottom of the turret. The lieutenant informed the captain that the pumps were disposing of the water and that the situation was under control, at least for the time being (fortunately, the ammunition was safe and dry in the ship's magazine).

* * * * *

The hours crawled by while the turbulent seas washed over us and water rushed through the eye-slits with increasing force. Near the hour of four I made my way down to the engine room to record the state of the engines.

The engineers, their faces grim with worry, were grouped near the ship's boilers. During the past several hours, waves had broken over the openings of the pipes of the ventilation system—the pipes that supplied our ship with air. The engineers were troubled because some seawater had leaked down the pipes into the ventilation system. The danger was instantly clear—if the belts of the ventilation system became waterlogged they could slip from their tracks and the engines would fail. The engineers were aware of the danger. Soon, every man on board the ship knew of our peril, and for the first time I sensed uneasiness amongst the crew.

The surge of water continued, relentlessly. Another uneasy hour passed; the minutes dragging slowly, second by second, as we anxiously watched water dripping into the ventilation belts. Eventually, what we feared would happen, happened. The belts absorbed too much water and slipped off their tracks. Immediately, our supply of fresh air was choked off. Almost at once the air inside the ironclad felt thick, stale, like the air in a walled-up tomb.

There was sufficient air for breathing, at least for the time being, but the fires in the boilers needed an abundant supply of air to keep its fuel of coal burning hot. Within minutes the fire in the boilers burned lower and lower; the color of the flames changing from blue-white to yellow. A few minutes later, the engines, starved for its fuel of hot-burning coal, groaned to a stop.

The silence on the ship was the silence of the grave. In that deathly silence I swear I heard the wild beating of each man's heart. My own heart thrashed painfully against my chest as the engine room filled with the stink of poisonous coal gas.

First Assistant Engineer Isaac Newton and Chief Engineer Alban Stimers darted over to the boilers, but their efforts to stoke up the coals were in vain.

Other engineers, sailors, and firemen, crowded into the room, but the situation seemed hopeless, impossible. We covered our noses and mouths with our hands as we labored to fan air into the coals, but one by one we were overcome by the poison.

I collapsed near the boiler. I felt as limp as a child's rag doll; I couldn't move; I couldn't turn my head or speak. Desperately, I struggled to keep my eyes open, for I knew that once they closed I would die. The seconds of my struggle seemed endless, agonizingly endless, but finally I gave up and closed my eyes . . .

Chapter Twelve

Even while I prepared to die, I heard men shouting and felt hands snatching at my clothes and dragging me across the wet floor. My head was exploding with pain and nausea gripped my stomach like a vise. I forced my eyes open again, but I only saw the floor as I was being carried through a corridor, up a hatchway and over the top of the turret.

I laid without moving, satisfied to simply stare at the clouds scudding across the sky. The sea air smelled wonderful, more wonderful than I had ever remembered and I gulped great breaths of that sweet smelling stuff. Around me, as far as the eye could see, stretched endless miles of grey water tipped with white caps. I laid still, comfortably content, despite the chill of the wind that cut through my wet clothes and the salt water that stung my face. Near me laid two other men; both were still unconscious, though I could see by the rising of their chests that they were drinking in the air with as much greed as I.

The three of us had been placed on top of the turret, the only spot on the ship above water where a man could sit without being swept into the sea. After the other two men had awoken, we climbed back down the hatchway into the ironclad.

Below, in the engine room, the air had cleared enough for the engineers and firemen to work on the ventilation system, but another problem had arisen from the low-burning coal fires: a drop in the boiler pressure had stopped the steam pumps that pumped excess water back into the ocean. The engineers were using hand pumps in a frantic attempt to pump out seawater.

I manned one of the pumps and we pumped until the muscles in our arms burned, and yet, no matter how hard we pumped, we could not force the water up the turret's tower. As the water level in the hull deepened we quietly accepted the possibility that we could drown inside the ship, and yet not a man aboard that ship spoke of that possibility.

Miraculously, when all looked lost, the tugboat changed direction and began to tow us towards land. Five long hours passed before we reached smooth waters, but as night began its descent, the winds dropped and the engineers revived the engines.

* * * * *

The next five hours were spent in calm water which greatly renewed the crew's confidence in our ship—in spite of the fact that water had to be pumped from the hull, that the ventilation system had to be dried and put in order, and that water leaks had to be plugged. The crew worked without complaint even though they lacked time for food or sleep. I believe they were satisfied just to be alive.

Around midnight, while the ship passed over a shoal, I took a moment to crouch down in a corridor to record additional information in the notebook.

All of a sudden the ship twisted in the water; the notebook flew from my hands as I was thrown to the floor. The *Monitor* had re-entered rough waters. I snatched up the notebook, pushed it into my one dry pocket and braced myself as the ship turned and pitched like a wild stallion put to saddle. Above us, above the waves, the winds shrieked and echoed eerily down the tower.

An alarm was sent up—the cables of wire that ran from the ship's rudder to the steering wheel had slipped off their guidewheels. The *Monitor* was out of control, pitching forward, lurching sideways, slapping wave after wave after wave . . .

Struggling to keep my balance, I pulled myself up the ladder leading to the pilothouse. Captain Worden stood at the wheel, trying to steer the ship into the waves.

Seeing me he shouted, "Find Higgins and Clarke. Tell them to climb out on top of the turret to signal the *Seth Low* for assistance. We will founder if we don't reach calm waters."

I did as he asked and moments later the two sailors were climbing up the hatchway while the crew and I waited anxiously in the corridors below. Howling winds whipped down the tower; the winds told us what none of us wanted to say out loud: Higgins and Clarke could be swept into the raging sea.

While the two sailors were risking their lives in the raging winds, I regretted for the third time that day that Mr. Ericsson hadn't had time to install his system for visual signalling between the *Monitor* and the *Seth Low*. Indeed, our only method of communication with the tugboat was through shouting—a primitive method at best. I flipped open the notebook to write a note about the vital need for a signalling system when a sailor called out, "They're coming in."

The captain left his helmsman at the wheel and was at the foot of the hatchway when Higgins and Clarke clambered down the rungs. Both men were drenched and clearly exhausted from battling the waves and winds. The short climb down the ladder had taxed their remaining strength and they dropped to their hands and knees, heaving and panting for breath. Higgins gasped, "We had to cling to the tower . . . to keep from being washed overboard . . ." Then pushing to his feet, he saluted Captain Worden and reported, "Sir, we failed to alert the *Seth Low*. The wind blew away our voices . . . and sir, the towline looks strained . . . it looks close to breaking . . ."

I clenched my jaw.

If the towline snapped between our ship and the tugboat, the master of the *Seth Low* wouldn't notice our separation until it was too late to rescue us. Unnoticed, the *Monitor* would founder in the rough waters until the weight of our iron plates dragged us to the depths of the sea.

If the towline snapped, every man on our ship would drown . . .

Chapter Thirteen

I thought there would be some panic amongst the crew, but instead those brave men acquired almost serene faces. No one said a word. What could be said when you believe that you're trapped within an iron coffin and awaiting certain death?

Two engineers, their names I have since forgotten, were determined not to die. They bent over the steering gear and though perspiration slid down into their eyes like heavy rain, they managed, somehow, to affix the steering gear back on its track. Immediately, the *Monitor*'s wild lurches and pitches were calmed.

Another sailor was sent above to check the towline and the grin on his face when he returned told us the good news: the cables between the *Seth Low* and our ship had held fast. None of us minded, then, our tiresome chore of plugging the leaks. We knew that the *Monitor* was a ship that could battle a turbulent sea and win.

No one slept during the remaining hours of night, and when daylight showed through the eye-slits,

Clarke was ordered to go above and signal the *Seth Low* to tow us towards land. As our ship turned landward, we entered peaceful waters and all of us, to the very last man, sighed with relief. Around eight that morning Cook called us to breakfast; dried biscuits, of course, but, to us the meal seemed like a feast for we had survived the longest night of our voyage.

Over twelve hours later, at approximately four in the afternoon, the *Monitor* reached the entrance of the Chesapeake Bay. The crew cheered, but then silence settled on the ship, for we heard the booming of heavy guns. Somewhere, in the near distance, a battle was being waged.

Chapter Fourteen

We headed in a westward direction for the final thirty miles of our voyage to Hampton Roads, the site of our federal fleet. With each passing mile we listened to the roar of cannons as we hazarded wild guesses about what lay ahead. As a precautionary measure, Captain Worden ordered the *Monitor* stripped for battle. So, while we were still under tow by the *Seth Low*, the canvas shelter that had protected the turret during the sea voyage was taken off and stowed below. As well, the funnels and blower pipes were removed and stowed on top of the canvas.

A federal tugboat met us while we stood ten miles off Fort Monroe; the tug master reported grim news: the *Merrimack* had sunk the U.S.S. *Cumberland* and had reduced the U.S.S. *Congress* to surrender. None of us wanted to accept the fact that we had arrived too late to stop the *Merrimack*, but we were a sombre lot of men as we neared Hampton Roads and saw the *Congress* burning on the water. We knew that the Confederates had unleashed a monster called the *Merrimack*.

Night approached its ninth hour when we drew up alongside the fleet's flagship, the frigate U.S.S. *Roanoke*. Immediately, a messenger brought written orders that the *Monitor* should offer protection to the U.S.S. *Minnesota*, for she had grounded herself at Newport News. The *Merrimack* had already attacked her once and was expected to return in the morning to destroy the defenseless ship. Captain Worden was provided a local pilot, a clever man who was familiar with the waters of Hampton Roads (reportedly, he could spot a sandbar from a thousand yards away) and as soon as the cables connecting us to the *Seth Low* were cast off, we set course for Newport News. For the first time that entire voyage, the *Monitor* moved under her own power.

Near two in the morning, we spotted the ship, the *Congress*. She stood in the water, burning like a giant torch; the blazing light cast off by her fire guided us towards the *Minnesota*.

The 50-gun steam frigate, *Minnesota*, lay grounded in mud; several tugboats had attached wire cables to her sides in an attempt to pull her free. We soon learned that during her battle yesterday, the strong recoil of the *Minnesota*'s own broadsides had pushed her hull deep into mud. As a student of engineering I understood at once that the *Minnesota* had created a vacuum of her own making—a powerful vacuum that had sucked the ship into the mud.

When we pulled alongside the *Minnesota*, Lieutenant Greene went aboard ship to inform the commander, Captain Van Brunt, that the *Monitor* would shield her from further attacks. Supposedly, Van Brunt was much relieved, for he was certain the *Merrimack* would return by morning to destroy his ship. If she did return, she would be greeted by an unpleasant surprise: our mighty ironclad, the U.S.S. *Monitor*. As far as we knew, the Confederates were still unaware of the *Monitor*'s presence in Hampton Roads.

* * * * *

Most of us took advantage of our ship being at rest by stretching out on the deck. The sky above was lit up by small stars and though it was only the beginning of March the air was comfortable, though cool. We sat under that canopy of stars in quiet, for we were weary though unwilling to go below to sleep. Our need for sleep was disturbed by the awful sight of the *Congress* burning on the water. Few of us spoke, which measured our weariness, and complete silence overcame us when a launch drew up beside our ship; it was Lieutenant Greene returning from the U.S.S. *Minnesota*.

At the very moment that the lieutenant stepped aboard our ship, the night exploded around us. I stared across the water as a great ball of fire swelled upwards, lighting up the entire sky so that the stars, themselves, appeared to be on fire. Beneath the fiery sky loomed a monstrous shadow on the water, a shadow that had once been a ship. The U.S.S. *Congress* had exploded.

Clouds of grey-black smoke billowed out as wood, iron and human flesh splattered like a gruesome rain over the water. The smoke dimmed the stars; the awful rain discolored the waters; and the acrid smells of fire and smoke and death tainted the river's breeze.

Somehow, I knew that all of us shared the same thought: the *Merrimack* had to be destroyed.

Chapter Fifteen

That night was far from over. Two hours after the midnight hour, Captain Worden and Lieutenant Greene received several visitors on board: the master of the federal tugboat, *Zouave*, and the pilot of the U.S.S. *Cumberland*. Both men looked fatigued as they sat on folding chairs placed in the turret. I was permitted to attend the interview in order to continue my note taking for Mr. Ericsson.

The master of the *Zouave*, a worn, sad-faced fellow named Henry Reany, sat with his cap on his lap and his head lowered. He spoke without looking at anyone; his voice sounded as sad as his face. He said, "Yesterday started out bright, clear and calm . . . our fleet swung on their anchors not expecting trouble . . . indeed, most of the ships had wet laundry hanging on the riggings." He paused and looked up at the captain before saying, "There were several vessels anchored off Fort Monroe—some gun boats and the frigates, *St. Lawrence*, *Minnesota* and *Roanoke*. Seven miles to the southwest, at Newport News, both the sloop *Cumberland* and the frigate *Congress* stood at anchor."

His sorrowful eyes remained on the sympathetic face of Captain Worden when he said, "My crew finished their morning duties early . . . by the hour of eleven . . . so we tied up at the wharf to eat our noon meal. Afterwards, my quartermaster spotted billows of smoke on the Elizabeth River. We cut our lines from the wharf and pulled alongside the *Cumberland* and received orders to identify the ship approaching from Norfolk. We departed at once . . . two miles out we saw an odd-looking vessel that resembled the roof of a barn with a chimney that was spilling out great mounds of smoke. We couldn't tell at first what the odd craft was until my boatswain's mate made out the rebel's flag and we knew the *Merrimack* was on the move. I made the decision to begin the action and ordered my crew to quarters. We opened our 30-pounder Parrott gun at that strange vessel, but she made no response. We fired again and again until six shots had been spent, but she ignored our fire. At that point the recall flag was raised on the *Cumberland* signalling my boat's return to her side.

"During our return trip, the *Congress* went to quarters and fired on the *Merrimack* as did our shore batteries at Newport News. The *Merrimack* moved through the waters, ignoring her attackers, until she stood side by side with the *Congress*. It was then that the rebel's ironclad fired her guns at both the *Congress* and the *Cumberland*. By the time my tug reached the *Cumberland* she had begun to fire on the *Merrimack*."

The pilot of the *Cumberland*, A. B. Smith, interrupted the master by saying, "When I first saw the approach of the *Merrimack* I thought she looked like a giant crocodile. She was a strange sight to behold with her sides of iron and her ports fixed with guns. The iron ram at her prow was pointing forward just above the surface of the water. That crocodile wore an iron skin . . . we soon learned that no amount of fire could split that iron skin. Our cannonballs bounced off her sides as though we had fired balls of India rubber. One of our balls split the *Merrimack*'s flagstaff which brought down her Confederate colors, but otherwise our cannonballs bothered her less than a swarm of flies."

Mr. Smith grew silent for a moment, as though struggling with the pain of his memories, before saying, "The *Cumberland* fired at least six or eight broadsides before the *Merrimack* opened fire at us. One of her shots . . . only one, mind you . . . killed five of our Marines. Those poor men were torn to pieces . . . their arms and legs and heads separated from the trunks of their bodies . . . flesh and bones covered our decks . . . the blood ran so freely that one of our ship's firemen slipped in the blood and fell headlong overboard."

He paused again, his memories overcame him and we waited quietly until he said, "It was an impossible task to steer my ship out of harm's way and so we waited helplessly as the *Merrimack* smashed her iron ram into our side . . . the force of her blow drove us back upon our anchors . . . that one blow tore a hole in the hold of our ship . . . a hole so wide that if five tall men stood shoulder to shoulder, they could have walked through that hole at the same time."

The pilot clasped his hands together and again paused in the telling of his story. I studied his face; he was clenching his teeth. We waited until he could go on and finally he said in a lowered voice, "Even while water swept into that hole, the *Merrimack*'s broadsides blew apart the crew of my ship. Men I thought of as brothers were killed or maimed beyond description and yet those brave men kept cheering for our Union. Cheers that came from their hearts. Even as the forward part of the ship caught on fire, the cheering continued. Some of their cheers changed into death rattles that caught in their throats . . ."

Captain Worden leaned over and placed a comforting hand on the shoulder of the grief-stricken man and after some time Mr. Smith continued, "The fire was put out, but the water was filling up the hold and pouring into the ports. The weight of the water was pulling the bow of the ship into the deep. At some point, a sailor on the *Merrimack* appeared on her roof and one of our gunners shot him. Split him into two halves. We never saw another rebel after that. They were smart to stay safe inside their iron crocodile, for the gunners of my ship were filled with rage. My crew fired continuously, even though our guns had no effect. And yet . . . and yet . . . though the *Merrimack* only shot at us on occasion, each one of their shells hit my ship and struck down my crew. Within one hour my ship was destroyed. Within one hour my crew was slaughtered."

Captain Worden interjected a question at that point. He asked, "Do I understand you to mean that the *Merrimack* turned her guns on two ships at one time?"

"Yes, sir," Mr. Smith said. "The *Merrimack* had positioned herself between both ships, the *Cumberland* and the *Congress*, and throughout that hour she fired her broadsides at each of us in turn. Both ships were clearly within point-blank range of her guns."

Mr. Smith stood up then, and standing with his back against the wall he said, "The *Merrimack* has to be stopped. You cannot imagine what the deck of my ship looked like . . . it was littered with torn and bleeding bodies. The ship's surgeon and his assistants tried to attend the wounded, but under enemy fire, it was an impossible situation. By then water had flooded into the after-magazine, but some of my crew still refused to abandon their posts in the shell room . . . some of those brave lads drowned. When the water crept up to the main gun-deck the order was given that each man should save himself, but several gunners refused, even then, to give up. One of those gunners, a courageous man named Matthew Tenney, manned gun number seven. Even though gun number six was submerged under water, Matthew stayed at his position and fired and then, because he was a small man, he must have thought he could escape when his port opened with the recoil of his gun . . . but when Matthew started to climb through, water rushed in with such force that he was thrown back and drowned.

"By then, men were jumping through portholes or trying to reach the spar-deck by forcing their way through companionways, but many, so many of our crew, were unable to escape . . . many, too many . . . went down with the ship."

Again, Mr. Smith sat down. Exhaustion and sadness showed in his eyes as he said, "I am proud to report that none of the survivors were captured by the enemy. Some of the crew, including myself, managed to escape into the water. Some were rescued by small boats, but others tried to swim ashore and . . . drowned . . ."

He choked on the word drowned, and Henry Reany finished by saying, "When the *Cumberland* sank, our nation's flag was still flying as the ship disappeared beneath the water. Deep below that very spot are sands fifty or fifty-five feet beneath the water—the very same height of the ship. When the *Cumberland* sank she must have lodged herself on those sands because even now, you can see the *Cumberland*'s pennant still attached to her topmast, waving above the water. That flag marks the water grave of a grand ship and an honorable crew."

Chapter Sixteen

Captain Worden shook the hands of the two men and said, "I greatly appreciate your information. You have helped us prepare for tomorrow's battle."

The master of the tugboat asked, "Sir, would it suit your purposes to speak to a member of the crew of the *Congress*?"

"It would indeed," Captain Worden replied and before the hour had passed Lieutenant Austin Pendergrast, the second in command of the U.S.S. *Congress*, was asking permission to come aboard.

Permission granted, he stepped from the side of the tugboat *Zouave* onto the deck of the *Monitor*. The night air was fresh and Captain Worden conducted the next interview under the stars.

Lieutenant Pendergrast spoke in a clear, loud voice that carried across the deck of the *Monitor*. He said, "My ship, the U.S.S. *Congress*, served as the target for several Confederate ships. The *Merrimack* shot shells that struck us both fore and aft, and at the same time a small rebel steamer fired constantly at our starboard quarter. Two other rebel vessels, the

Patrick Henry and the *Jamestown*, steamed up from the James River and fired a steady barrage at us. My ship was attacked by four enemy ships at one time and we had only one line of defense: two guns mounted on our stern. Both guns were useless. The gunners who had manned them were dead. Decapitated by the rebel's shells. I found the severed heads of my men . . . on the deck beneath their guns."

Swallowing hard, Lieutenant Pendergrast sat up stiffly and continued, "Our ship was doomed. Our commander, Captain Joseph Smith, was dead and our crew had been hacked to pieces by shells. Our guns were demolished—our only hope for assistance was the *Minnesota*. Unfortunately, she had grounded herself in mud. I had no choice. I yielded to the enemy, hauled down the ship's colors, and surrendered."

Lieutenant Pendergrast cleared his throat noisily and said, "As soon as our colors were lowered, the rebel's gunboats *Beaufort* and *Raleigh* came alongside and I surrendered to Lieutenant Parker of the *Beaufort*.

"When the Confederates boarded my ship they were clearly shocked by the carnage they had caused. One of their officers walked across the deck towards me. Before he reached the railing where I stood, I heard him sob, 'Dear God, my shoes are covered with their brains and blood.' Some of the rebel sailors disobeyed direct orders to board my ship. They couldn't bring themselves to step on the arms or legs or heads that littered the deck. They refused to step into the blood that spread like a river of red . . ."

It was fitting that the interview was being conducted in the dark. Although Lieutenant Pendergrast spoke without hesitation I could tell by the tormented tone of his voice that his eyes were wet.

Without pausing though, he said, "The wounded of my crew moaned with pain: men with stomachs split open so that their guts spilled out, men with arms wrenched from their sockets, men with legs ripped half off, and men with scorched faces. Their cries were heard by the Confederates as well, for several rebel officers and sailors came aboard to offer assistance to my wounded men. I was grateful for their charity.

"Not too surprisingly, our federal forces on shore ignored my decision to surrender my ship. In an attempt to keep the rebels from taking possession of the *Congress*, our land batteries shelled the enemy's vessels; two officers on the gunboat, *Raleigh*, were blown apart and other rebels were killed while they were ministering to the wounded on my ship. Some of my own sailors were accidently killed by Union fire.

"The Confederates soon tired of being shot at and they retreated back to their ships. They took thirty of my men as prisoners. As soon as the rebels deserted the *Congress*, I ordered my remaining crew to escape. Some climbed into small boats; others jumped overboard and swam ashore. The white flag still flew on the mast when my crew abandoned ship."

Lieutenant Pendergrast continued in his loud voice, "I was the last one to leave the *Congress*. I was fortunate enough to make my escape on a small craft and even more fortunate to have taken my spyglass with me. The sun was blinding by then, but I was able to see the commodore standing on the deck of the *Merrimack*. I watched as he gestured wildly at his crew and moments later I saw hot-shot fly from the ironclad towards the deck of my ship. Those rebels were determined to burn the *Congress* before the Union could reclaim her. While the *Merrimack* threw hot-shot, the federal shore batteries shot at the *Merrimack,* striking down her commodore and one sailor. They fell wounded, though I believe not fatally, and sailors swarmed up onto the deck and carried the two men back inside the ironclad."

Lieutenant Pendergrast paused in the telling of his story to say, "The commodore of the *Merrimack* appeared to be grievously wounded—in my opinion, he was wounded seriously enough to be replaced by his second in command."

The news of a possible change in command was interesting, but since no one could identify the officers who commanded the *Merrimack*, the subject wasn't worth further discussion.

Lieutenant Pendergrast returned to his story by saying, "After I had reached shore I again peered through my glass. Beyond my burning ship I saw the ironclad and rebel gunboats encircle the *Minnesota*. Because the *Minnesota* was still grounded I assumed she would suffer the same fate that had befallen my ship. There was nothing more I could do except watch and pray.

"The noise of cannon fire was terrible to hear. I strained to see, but with the smoke swirling up from the discharged shells and the darkness of early night it was difficult to see clearly. I could see a large hole in the *Minnesota*'s side, but she was grounded so in no danger of sinking. Through my glass I watched as sailors fell from her sides as a fire burst out which sent sailors scuttling for water buckets. That fire was quickly quenched, but I presumed the *Minnesota* was still doomed.

"Then, quite unexpectedly, the rebel's ironclad turned about and steamed away towards our two ships, the *Roanoke* and the *St. Lawrence*. Earlier, both ships had been grounded, but they had floated off and were being towed to safety. The *Merrimack* pursued those ships like a hungry sea shark until something brought her about, for she turned again and steamed off in the direction of Norfolk. Perhaps the fall of night and the ebbing of the tides sent that ravenous shark scurrying back to its anchorage."

I sat on the deck for a long while after Lieutenant Pendergrast had gone ashore, and after our commodore, Captain Worden, and his second in command, Lieutenant Greene, had retired below. I doubt either officer slept. I doubt any of our crew slept during those few hours that remained of night. And yet, as I sat under the star-glazed skies and looked over the water towards Norfolk I knew, somehow, that the crew of the *Merrimack* slept as soundly as babes. I knew, too, that they dreamt dreams of victory.

Chapter Seventeen

In the early morning hours of Sunday, March 9, our ship lay hidden behind the *Minnesota*; it was certain that the *Merrimack* would return to finish destroying the *Minnesota*. We would wait in her shadow until the rebel's ironclad closed up within a mile range before we attacked.

Lieutenant Greene took me aside to underline my duty during the upcoming battle: to keep detailed notes of every aspect of the ship's operation while under enemy fire. I would have access to every part of the ship—in the turret, to determine if the gun-tower revolved successfully—in the pilot-house, to determine if there was ample protection, if it was located in the right spot, and if the eye-slits were adequate for spying—in the engine room, to note if the engines worked efficiently—and in the port areas, to determine if the ports closed properly after the guns fired and if the platforms absorbed the recoil of the fired guns.

None of us felt rested enough for battle. We were an exhausted crew without a single hour of sleep in the past two days. We were a hungry crew with nothing more than dried biscuits in our stomachs since our departure from New York. And we were a tense crew, for none of us knew with certainty if the *Monitor*'s iron coat could protect us from the mighty *Merrimack*. And yet, not a single man revealed a coward's heart as we waited for the *Merrimack*.

I spent those hours of waiting in the pilothouse. My stomach ached with hunger, but I couldn't force down another hard biscuit. My mouth felt dry, my hands were wet and clammy, for I had never been through a battle. It seemed to me as I waited for battle that time had stopped, for each minute crept by like an eternity of its own. I was anxious for the battle to begin, and yet, just as anxious to stand there with only my thoughts to trouble me.

I thought of Julia—the way the sun had changed the color of her hair, the sound of her laughter, the sweetness of her kiss, our only kiss. I thought of how carefully she had studied my eyes. How she had compared their color to her mother's amber brooch, the brooch she'd wear until my return. And I thought of how she had smiled when she said that my eyes were the eyes of a dreamer. How had she known that I had always been a dreamer? Dreams of beautiful ships, and now, dreams of a beautiful maiden named Julia.

And I thought, too, of my parents, of my mother's gentle voice and my father's quiet wisdom. Surely, they would have welcomed Julia as my wife, for I still intended to send Julia the letter proposing marriage. Even as I checked my pocket to see if the letter was safe, I heard Captain Worden shout, "Gentlemen, to quarters. The smoke of our enemy has been sighted."

Chapter Eighteen

I rushed into the engine room and opening the notebook I wrote:

> *The crew is preparing for attack. The engineers have stoked up the coals in the boilers to ensure there is enough steam. The* Monitor *must depend on her speed while battling the enemy ship.*

I then made my way to the turret, where sixteen, strong-armed men were standing by our two guns. No one spoke. Absolute silence was necessary to hear the captain's orders. Lieutenant Greene, who commanded the turret, stood by his gunners; the lieutenant's face wore an odd expression as though he were somewhere else, far away. I whispered, "Sir, is there a problem with the guns?" He shook his head and bending his head close to me he whispered back, "I was just thinking about the strangeness of life. I have learned that an old friend, my former roommate at the Naval Academy, is serving aboard the *Merrimack*. I never thought I'd be firing at a friend with only one thought in mind—to blast him out of the water."

Having said that, he seemed to shake his thoughts away and turning towards the sixteen gunners, he again broke the silence to say, "Lads, the shoreline is crowded with people: hundreds of our fellow sailors, soldiers and civilians waiting to witness a battle between two ironclads. No doubt they believe our ship is too tiny to defeat the giant *Merrimack*, but we'll prove them wrong. We will defeat her. Then, those watching will tell their children and grandchildren that they witnessed David's defeat of Goliath."

The gunners grinned at their lieutenant and returned to their posts. They were a powerful lot of men; their arms were thick with the muscles that would be needed to man the heavy guns. The guns were eleven-inch Dahlgren guns, oddly-shaped cannons that resembled bottles. They were the finest naval weapons our navy possessed.

Mr. Ericsson had built a special platform beneath each gun. The platforms would absorb the recoil caused by the firing of the guns. Recoil could put a hole in a ship or kill a gunner. The gunners knew that, but they shared my faith that Mr. Ericsson's platform design would protect them.

I stepped back and watched Lieutenant Greene peering outside through an eye-slit. During the battle he would have to sight the *Merrimack* through a very narrow area between the edges of the port and the gun barrels. Then, while the turret was still revolving and the *Monitor* was still in motion, he would pull on a lanyard, a strong-braided rope, to fire the guns. To make his task more difficult, he would have to avoid firing towards the *Monitor*'s pilothouse, for it sat only fifty feet forward of the turret.

I wondered if the lieutenant was checking the visibility of the white chalk marks he had scrawled on the deck the previous night. White marks that indicated the ship's four directions: starboard (right-hand side of the ship); port (the left-hand side of the ship); stern (the rear of the ship); and bow (the front section of the ship). Lieutenant Greene would need those directional marks during the battle for accurate aiming and firing of the guns (I wrote a suggestion in the notebook that Mr. Ericsson should paint white directional markers on the decks of his ironclads).

I hurried to the pilothouse where Captain Worden, his pilot and a helmsman waited as the *Merrimack* slowly approached the *Minnesota*. There was barely enough room for the three of them in the pilothouse, but the helmsman and pilot were small men, so there was a narrow margin of space for me to stand while I made observations.

The pilothouse was perhaps the most danger-ous spot on the ship in spite of the fact that Mr. Ericsson had used bars of iron, twelve inches thick, to build the walls of the house. Dangerous, because the pilothouse would be exposed to enemy fire from its position forward on the deck.

The air in the pilothouse was stale with the smell of perspiration and sea-salted clothes; it was, after all, nothing more than a small iron box rising five feet above the deck (the floor dropped a few feet so we could stand without stooping).

Captain Worden was peering through an eye-slit. It seemed incredible to me that during the battle he would have to stay pressed against the wall, peer-ing through a tiny hole to con, or direct, his helms-man. I watched the captain as he turned his face just a fraction towards a voice tube that connected him with the turret's tower. "Lieutenant Greene," he shouted, "the smoke trail of our enemy grows thicker . . . it appears that the crew of the *Minnesota* has gone to quarters." There was a brief reply by the lieutenant and then Captain Worden returned to the eye-slit to study the situation outside.

I stood quietly, waiting and watching the captain as he, in turn, waited and watched through the eye-slit, when of a sudden, he jerked back and barked into the voice tube, "Gentlemen, the *Merrimack* has been sighted. She is fast approaching the *Minnesota*. Man your stations and prepare for battle." As the *Monitor* slowly moved forward, I heard Captain Worden murmur, "And God help us all."

Chapter Nineteen

At that very moment any fears I felt earlier evaporated with the sheer excitement of what lay ahead. I am sure if I had thought logically about what a naval battle involved, I would have been somewhat frightened, but my thoughts circled around Mr. Ericsson's ingenious ironclad, the U.S.S. *Monitor*. Had he designed a ship that could defeat the *Merrimack*? Would his turret revolve properly? Would his iron plates shield the ship from cannon-balls? Would his two guns equal the *Merrimack*'s ten guns? Would his platforms absorb the guns' recoil? Last night, Lieutenant Greene mentioned that the captain of the *Minnesota* had compared the *Merrimack* to a giant and the *Monitor* to a pygmy. Could a pygmy defeat a giant?

Captain Worden, keeping watch through his eye-slit, shouted through the voice tube, "Gentlemen, we have rounded the *Minnesota* and are moving full steam ahead towards the enemy. Our goal is to engage the *Merrimack* and her escort of enemy vessels as far away as possible from the *Minnesota*."

Then a moment later Captain Worden shouted, "The *Merrimack*'s escort is deserting her. She is alone. She is firing . . ."

A sound, terrible to hear, surrounded us; it was the sound of enemy shells howling above us, exploding in the waters around us. Another broadside of cannonballs hit our ship before the captain yelled through the voice tube, "Gentlemen, commence firing."

Without hesitation I ran back to the turret, determined to watch Lieutenant Greene fire the first shot. Just as I entered the tower a broadside struck the *Monitor*; the vibration threw me against the wall, but I regained my footing as another round of cannonballs hit us. The cannonballs clanged noisily against our ship, but the armored plates were undamaged. We were safe within our cocoon of iron. If any of us had harbored doubts about the *Monitor*, those doubts were gone in that instant. Our tiny ship was equal to the mighty *Merrimack*.

The gunners hoisted a shell that weighed 175 pounds and loaded it into the mouth of a gun. Carefully, Lieutenant Greene sighted his target; he squinted his eyes, concentrating as the tower slowly turned before pulling on the lanyard and firing the heavy gun.

The discharge of the gun was deafening. Grinning, I pulled out my notebook and wrote:

. . . at the moment of discharge the iron plate dropped over the open port providing adequate protection for the gunners as they prepare the gun for another discharge . . .

A moment later I wrote:

. . . the platform absorbed the recoil of the heavy guns as designed. The gunners are in no personal danger from firing their own guns . . .

I took out my pocket watch and timed the gunners—in the notebook I wrote:

. . . Seven minutes—seven minutes are required to fully load each gun, to sight the target, to set the tower in motion, to stop the tower if necessary, to pull on the lanyard and fire . . .

Seven long minutes and throughout those seven minutes the guns of the *Merrimack* fired upon our ship continuously.

* * * * *

The gunners depended on every ounce of their vast strength to load and fire the heavy guns over and over again. Within the first hour of battle the heat in the tower greatly increased, and drenched with perspiration, the gunners ripped off their wet shirts. Two sailors were promptly ordered to supply the tower with buckets of cool water.

Each blast of our guns deafened us, the smell of powder and smoke choked us, and thick soot covered us like a second skin, but each blast sounded like music to us. Strange, beautiful music. The gunners on the *Merrimack* made their own kind of music for the broadsides they fired at us rattled our teeth.

I was observing behind Lieutenant Greene when he turned to the voice tube and shouted, "Captain, where does the enemy bear?" There was no reply. Again the lieutenant shouted, "Where does the enemy bear?" Again only silence met his question and glancing over at me he said, "Mr. Hamiliton, find out why the captain is ignoring my calls."

I soon found the reason. The voice tube had broken; direct communication between the pilothouse and the turret was no longer possible. Captain Worden immediately assigned me and a crew member the task of carrying messages between him, the Captain, and Lieutenant Greene.

I took the first message to Lieutenant Greene:

The mile distance between us and the Merrimack *weakens the impact of our shells. I am steering directly towards the* Merrimack *until we stand within a hundred yards of her.*

Lieutenant Greene gave me a message for the Captain:

Once the turret tower begins to revolve, it is difficult to stop it or even reverse the movement in order to fire. Keep that information in mind when you give the enemy's bearings.

* * * * *

The firing continued. We loosened solid shot at the *Merrimack* and she answered with broadsides or grape shot that sounded like ice balls hitting our sides. After one especially jarring round of broadsides, Lieutenant Greene sent me running to the captain with an urgent question:

"In what direction does the Merrimack *bear?"*

The captain replied:

"The enemy bears to the port quarter."

That information didn't help Lieutenant Greene, for the directional chalk marks he had made on the deck had erased and he couldn't tell which direction the port quarter lay. To make matters worse, the motion of the ship and the revolving of the turret's tower had caused him and his gunners to lose their sense of direction. Lieutenant Greene shouted out his next message:

I have lost all sense of direction. The enemy is too far off for me to sight her with accuracy.

Can you approach so that I can sight the Merrimack *with my own eyes?*

Captain Worden agreed with the lieutenant's tactic. Bracing my feet, I stood beside him as he steered the *Monitor* directly towards the *Merrimack*.

Chapter Twenty

I stepped back and peered through an eye-slit in the wall of the pilothouse. Ahead, was the *Merrimack*, crouching in the water like a monstrous creature belching smoke. Slowly, she stood around and faced us, waiting at first as though to taunt us and then moving towards us with all the arrogance of a bully.

The distance between the *Merrimack* and our ship decreased with each passing minute. One mile. One-half mile. One-quarter mile. One thousand yards. One hundred yards. She fired upon us and I watched as the broadside hurled towards us. At that closeness, the broadside shook our ship, but though the iron plates rattled, they were left intact, undamaged.

Glancing over at me, Captain Worden bellowed, "Report to Lieutenant Greene. Tell him the *Merrimack* bears to our port."

I ran to the turret room, but there was no further need to relay directions to Lieutenant Greene. The nearness of our enemy made it possible for him to take his own bearings . . . he sighted . . . he aimed . . . he pulled on the lanyard . . . and he fired.

The *Merrimack* answered with a barrage of balls that hit the turret's tower. The clanging of iron cannonballs against the iron walls of our ship shook every bone in my body. I pressed the notebook against the turret's wall and trying to steady my hand I wrote:

> *Although the tower holds under direct fire, at close distance the impact . . .*

At that very moment another broadside hit the tower; I felt the concussion of the impact through the wall and fell to the floor, dazed. A gunner dragged me back from the wall and I laid nearly unconscious, my head spinning like a toy top.

I watched as a gunner, his face drooping with exhaustion, leaned back against the wall. I called out a warning, but it was too late. Another direct hit against the tower wall sent him sprawling to the floor. His eyes remained closed as he, too, was dragged over and placed beside me. I turned my head towards him; he wasn't dead for his chest rose with his breathing, but he was unconscious. I pushed myself into a sitting position and held my spinning head in my hands as the clanging, ringing, thudding noises of battle encompassed me.

Then, all at once our guns ceased firing. I pulled away my hands and shook my head trying to concentrate on the voices around me and eventually, through the haze of my dizziness, I heard the reason for the sudden silence: we had used up our ammunition. Our gunners had spent 43 projectiles.

Lieutenant Greene called for a messenger, but though I tried to raise myself up, my head had not yet cleared and dizziness brought me down again. A gunner stepped up to the lieutenant and took the message:

> *Lieutenant Greene needs fifteen minutes to transfer ammunition from the ship's magazine to the turret.*

Moments later the *Monitor* was turning away from the *Merrimack* towards open waters that were too shallow for the larger ironclad to enter.

The gunners filed out of the tower for much needed rest in the corridor, while sailors in the magazine lifted up ammunition through a hole in the tower's floor. As the crew rapidly worked, I pressed against the wall and pulled myself to my feet. My head had cleared somewhat, and so I was able to relay Lieutenant Greene's next message to the captain.

When I reached the pilothouse I found the captain looking through an eye-slit. "Captain Worden," I said, "Lieutenant Greene reports that the ammunition transfer will be completed in ten minutes."

He glanced at me before returning to the eye-slit and said in a flat voice, "That ten minutes may doom the *Minnesota*. The *Merrimack* is fast approaching her."

The helmsman, pilot and I each found our own eye-slits, and we watched the *Merrimack* as she moved slowly, but steadily, towards the *Minnesota*.

The *Minnesota*, though still aground in the mud, refused to wait like a rabbit in a trap; she opened up her cannons, firing broadsides at the *Merrimack*. Thick, black cannon smoke surrounded the frigate as her heavy guns fired continuously, but her barrage of cannonballs slid off the sides of the rebel's ironclad ship. I counted fifty or more broadsides, but they had no more effect on the ironclad than drops of rain.

The *Merrimack* closed in on the *Minnesota* and turning herself in the water so that she stood broadside of the frigate, that monstrous ironclad unleashed the fury of her guns.

Captain Worden cried out, "Ten minutes have passed . . . we are returning to battle." And taking the wheel he steered the *Monitor* from the shallows towards the ironclad, *Merrimack*.

Chapter Twenty-one

I watched through the eye-slit as we approached the *Merrimack*. While we bore down on her she turned slowly away from the *Minnesota* and faced us; then, picking up speed she aimed her iron bow at us. She came closer and closer, her intention clear—to ram us. Even though she had lost her iron ramming boot in the hull of the *Cumberland*, even though we sat too low in the water to be rammed, she meant to break us open.

My heart seemed to stop, my breathing grew jagged as I watched the *Merrimack* plow through the waters towards us. She was not a fast ship, but it seemed that she had sprouted wings. She closed in fast, looming up before us like a mammoth, ugly creature. Within seconds she would strike us, but in those seconds Captain Worden yanked hard on the helm and we slid by the *Merrimack*, narrowly escaping her deadly bow. As she passed us her stern scraped our ship; the sound was terrible to hear as though our skin had been scraped off our very bones.

Mere moments later, Captain Worden spun the wheel bearing towards the *Merrimack*'s after-quarter.

He muttered, "If only . . . we could . . . ram her rudder . . . we could cripple her steering gear," but his effort failed. The *Merrimack* glided away from our advance; we had missed her by a few feet.

I stayed at the eye-slit and watched in disbelief as the *Merrimack* turned and then slowed to a standstill. She had grounded herself in shoal water. Captain Worden pulled our ship astern of the *Merrimack* even as she struggled to free herself from the mud.

I rushed back to the turret room to learn how Lieutenant Greene's gunners would take advantage of our stationary target. I arrived to hear the lieutenant order the gunners to load shot, solid shot of 180 pounds. Precious minutes flew by as the gunners prepared the guns. There might only be enough time for one clear shot before the *Merrimack* freed herself, and so Lieutenant Greene took time to carefully sight his target—the stern of the *Merrimack*.

I stood back as he sighted, aimed and fired. The roar of the heavy gun deafened us even as we felt the vibrations of our direct hit.

Immediate word was sent down from the pilothouse that the shell had struck the *Merrimack*. I rushed up to the pilothouse and took my place at an eye-slit. Our shell had, indeed, hit the *Merrimack*'s stern; it had blasted off some of its iron plating and splintered a layer of wood. And yet, the *Merrimack* had not been opened. No hole was visible in her stern.

As if that shot had awoken a sleeping sea dragon, the *Merrimack* shook herself free from the mud and seemed to rise higher on the waves as she rode out into deeper waters.

Captain Worden handed over the wheel to his helmsman. Pressing his face against the wall, the captain peered through an eye-slit. "We will follow her to the ends of the earth," he muttered and then in a louder voice he called out directions as he conned the helmsman where to steer.

As our ship chased the rebel's ironclad I, too, remained at an eye-slit. It was difficult to see through the clouds of black smoke, but eventually the hideous shape of the *Merrimack* loomed before us.

Captain Worden soon made his intention clear: he intended to close up within a few yards of the enemy ship. I looked through the slit in the wall and marvelled at the size of the other ship; our dwarf-sized ship fit into her gigantic shadow. I stared at that enormous vessel and a loathing I have never known overwhelmed me. I hated the *Merrimack* for the destruction and death she had caused our fleet. She was my enemy, my country's enemy, and I watched her warily as one watches any blood-thirsty beast.

The ironclads stood so close to each other that my imagination overtook my senses. I imagined I could hear the *Merrimack*'s crew cursing at us. I imagined I could hear the beating of their happy hearts, for surely they expected to taste victory. And I imagined the hoarseness of their commander's voice when he shouted, "fire," as that monster ship spat a shell towards the very wall I stood behind.

The shell struck directly in front of my face. In that split second I saw the iron bars of the wall break apart and the roof above, partially lift open; in that split second, I felt the tremendous concussion of the blast as blood poured from my nose and ears and I was thrown backwards. My head struck the base of the steering wheel; the blow felt like the blow of a sledge hammer. I wrapped my arms around my head and closed my eyes against the pain. The blood on my face was warm; it flowed into my open mouth, gagging me, choking me. I spat out mouthfuls of blood and forced my eyes open.

Bright sunlight flooded through the damaged roof and yet the room was darkening with shadows. I stared up at Captain Worden; he looked as though he wore a ghoulish mask, for blood gushed from his forehead and dripped off his beard while his eyes were opened over-wide.

"My eyes," he cried out in a strangled voice, "I'm blind." He turned his bleeding face up towards the fierce sunlight. Perhaps the warmth of the sun renewed his composure, for his voice rang strong when he ordered the helmsman, "Sheer off into shallow water." Then, struggling across the small room, Captain Worden clutched at the sides of the ladder and climbed down.

I crawled towards the ladder to offer him assistance, if possible, but when I looked down, he was standing at the foot of the ladder, leaning his full weight against the rungs. At least I believe it was the captain, for the shadows were deepening and I could see very little despite the sunlight that filtered down the ladder.

My head ached from the blow. I closed my eyes. I heard familiar voices—the voices of Lieutenant Greene and Captain Worden and then I heard shuffling sounds as though someone was being half-carried, half-dragged down a corridor. A minute later I again heard the voice of Lieutenant Greene as he climbed up the ladder.

I opened my eyes and saw the lieutenant's face through a dark haze; he called me by name and when I didn't answer, he grabbed me under the arms and sat me up against the wall. Through a thickening fog of darkness, I watched as he took over the wheel and said to the helmsman, "Captain Worden was

Joy Renee Maine

confused in his blindness. The sudden explosion of light from the roof led him to believe the *Monitor* was seriously damaged and unfit for battle. We are only slightly damaged. Captain Worden has placed me in command. I am taking us back into battle."

After a short while I heard someone else (the pilot?) say, "Sir, the *Merrimack* is retreating towards the Elizabeth River. She appears to be headed back towards the Confederate's Navy Yard at Norfolk."

If Lieutenant Greene responded, I didn't hear his answer, but within seconds our guns opened up and fired and just as suddenly, the thunder of our guns ended. The battle of the ironclads was over.

My eyes closed and I felt myself drifting into sleep, but I refused to sleep and forced my eyes open. Darkness met me. I saw nothing. Nothing. I, too, had been blinded.

Chapter Twenty-two

Panic should have gripped me, but strangely I felt calm as I listened to the pilot direct Lieutenant Greene back towards the *Minnesota*. I suppose my calmness was caused by my belief that my vision would return before long, and so I felt content enough as the *Monitor* slid through the waters towards the frigate, *Minnesota*.

Even before our engines were shut down, I heard the noise of cheering, yelling, whistling and clapping sounds muffled, somewhat, by our ship's iron walls.

I was helped to my feet, guided through the ship and lifted over the side of the *Monitor* to the deck of the *Minnesota*. I heard, beside me, Captain Worden's voice as he, too, was put aboard the frigate. We were led through a mob of cheering, back-slapping sailors and lowered onto deck chairs; after hours inside the ironclad beneath the water, the sun on my face felt warm and reassuring. Under the hot sun I grew even more hopeful that my vision would soon be restored.

The ship's surgeon attended to us; he asked Captain Worden and me to describe what happened after the shell had struck the pilothouse, and then explained that he would have to wash the soot off our faces in order to examine our eyes. I heard water splashing into a basin and prepared to wait, for I assumed that Captain Worden would be examined first.

While the surgeon attended the Captain, I listened to the sounds of celebration surrounding me. The hundreds of sailors who manned the *Minnesota* were clearly overcome with joy and indeed they should have been. If it had not been for the *Monitor* the *Minnesota* would have been destroyed or captured. Their cheers sounded like a symphony to me, a wild symphony of jubilance, that grew even louder as the crew of the *Monitor* was welcomed aboard. After a time, I heard the familiar voice of Lieutenant Greene as he reported to Captain Worden, "The crew is aboard the *Minnesota*, sir. Every man is covered head to foot in black soot, but otherwise all are well and accounted for."

And I heard Captain Worden's response, "Thank God for that."

The news filled me with a mixture of emotions. Pride, that Mr. Ericsson's small ironclad had slain the giant *Merrimack* and saved Mr. Lincoln's fleet and his blockade of Southern ports. Relief, that none of our crew had perished in the battle. And anger, that in the final moments of conflict, Captain Worden and I had suffered injuries to our eyes.

After some time the surgeon told the Captain to hold his head as still as possible and a moment later he found the cause of the Captain's blindness. The explosion had thrown concrete dust into his eyes with tremendous force, burning his eyes.

Finally, the surgeon turned his attention to me. He wiped the blood from my ears, before washing my face and prodding the large bruise at the back of my head (though the bruise was painful, the skin was barely broken). At last, he began the slow task of cleaning my eyes. For several minutes his fingers probed the skin around my eyes, but he said he found nothing. No powder or soot or iron bits or flash-burns. Nothing that would have explained my blindness.

I knew, then, that I would never regain my sight. I sat, under the hot sun, and shivered as the warmth of the afternoon faded. I felt imprisoned in a cold world of darkness, a world from which there was no escape. I thought of my parents. I thought of Julia.

Julia. I remembered how the sun and the night's stars had illuminated her hair and eyes. I remembered the sorrow that had shadowed her beautiful face when we parted at the train station. And I remembered her whispered vow to wear her amber brooch until my return—the brooch that reminded her of my eyes.

My eyes. She had described my eyes as the eyes of a dreamer. I had dreamed once. Dreams of ships. Dreams of Julia. Those dreams belonged to a man who could see. Blind, I could never return to Harvard, or become a builder of ships. Blind, I could never marry Julia. I would never burden her with a useless husband.

I asked a sailor to guide me to the edge of the ship. Standing by the railing, I felt the icy spray of water against my face. I unbuttoned my pocket and pulled out the letter I had written to Julia. Then, even as I recalled the words of my marriage proposal, I tore up the letter and threw the pieces over the railing.

I couldn't see the bits of paper falling into the water, but in my mind's eye, I watched as each piece floated away with the tide.

Author's Note

The U.S.S. *Monitor* and the C.S.S. *Virginia* (*Merrimack*)

At the start of the Civil War in April 1861 the Union was forced to abandon the Federal Navy Yard in Norfolk, Virginia. One of the ships left behind was the steam frigate, the U.S.S. *Merrimack*, which was deliberately set on fire and sunk to prevent the Confederates from using the ship in their own navy.

However, the Confederates raised the ship, drained it of mud and determined that the hull and engine could be salvaged—with one major change: iron plates would be applied to transform the wooden frigate into an ironclad. When completed the ironclad would measure 263 feet in length, every inch covered with iron. The sloping citadel would be made of oak, 24 inches thick, with an additional covering of iron, two inches thick. The ship would be armed with four rifled guns (two 2-inchers and two 6.4-inchers) and six 9-inch smoothbores. In addition, the bow of the *Merrimack* would carry a 1,500-pound ramming prow of railroad iron. The ship, when afloat, would resemble the roof of a barn with a chimney blowing smoke.

Union spies eventually informed Mr. Lincoln about the ongoing reconstruction of the steam frigate into an ironclad. Lincoln and his advisors such as the Secretary of the Navy, Mr. Gideon Welles, immediately contracted the Swedish-born engineer and inventor, John Ericsson, to build an ironclad that could equal or defeat the *Merrimack* in battle.

Ericsson's genius design called for a hull that was flattened and covered with iron plates. The ship was unique in that it would float only a few feet above the water line, thus resembling a crocodile swimming beneath the surface of water. Ericsson purposely designed a small ship. Its small size allowed rapid movement through water and also provided a minute target for enemies to sight. Above the flattened hull of the ship were three projections: a round pilothouse which stood above the bow (forefront) of the ship; an iron-plated turret which stood nine feet above the middle of the ship; and a smokestack which stood above the stern (back end) of the ship. Although the ship only carried two 11-inch Dahlgren smoothbore cannons, the turret that housed the two guns could rotate in any direction. Thus, the cannons could be fired at any target from any position in the water. Once his ironclad was afloat, Ericsson christened the ship the U.S.S. *Monitor*.

By March of 1862 the Confederates' ironclad was afloat and ready for action. The Confederates re-christened their ironclad the C.S.S. *Virginia*, but she is remembered as the *Merrimack* (popular records incorrectly spell her name as *Merrimac* without the final letter "k").

On March 8 the *Merrimack* attacked the Union's blockading fleet in the waterway known as Hampton Roads, Virginia. The attack resulted in the sinking of the wooden ship, the 30-gun U.S.S. *Cumberland*, and the near devastation of the 50-gun wooden frigate

U.S.S. *Congress*. In turn, the federal ships' return of cannonballs fell like harmless raindrops against the iron sides of the *Merrimack*. Darkness ended that first day of battle. Only nightfall had saved the U.S.S. *Congress* from complete destruction.

The next morning, March 9, 1862, the Union awaited the *Merrimack*'s return with dread. If the U.S.S. *Congress* could be sunk it was probable that the remaining wooden vessels in the federal fleet would suffer the same fate. And, if the federal fleet in Hampton Roads was destroyed, Mr. Lincoln's blockade of southern ports would end. If that happened, the Confederacy could receive European imports of foodstuffs, cloth and other goods that the South desperately needed to win the war. On the morning of March 9 the Confederacy was confident that the blockade would soon end, and that confidence was based solely on their ironclad, the *Merrimack*.

That morning, March 9, the shoreline was crowded with spectators who wished to watch the giant *Merrimack* continue her destructive path down Hampton Roads. The *Merrimack* moved steadily towards the U.S.S. *Congress* who lay grounded and helpless, but as the giant ironclad approached the defenseless ship, the crowds watched in amazement as a tiny, flattened ship moved around the *Congress* towards the *Merrimack*. That tiny ship was the *Monitor*. Unbeknownst to the Confederates, the Union's *Monitor* had reached Hampton Roads on the evening of March 8 and had hidden itself behind the U.S.S *Congress* to launch a surprise attack on the *Merrimack*.

The battle lasted for hours without either ship gaining the advantage even though the ironclads closed in and fired direct shots within yards of each other. The *Merrimack* made several attempts to ram the *Monitor*, but the federal commander, Captain L. Worden, used his ship's speed to outmaneuver the slower ship. Both ironclads took numerous direct hits, but neither crew was endangered, for the iron plates covering both ships offered remarkable protection from cannonballs and shot. At one point the *Merrimack* suffered a direct blow that cracked Its side and at battle's end the *Monitor*'s captain was blinded by a shell that exploded in front of the eye-slit he was peering through. Still, by the time the battle ended after the noon hour, there was no clear winner although both sides claimed victory. Perhaps the Union had the greater claim to victory because the federal fleet had been saved and thus Mr. Lincoln's blockade could continue to cripple the South's war effort.

The *Monitor*'s commander, Captain Worden, was moved to Washington, D.C. for treatment of his injured eyes. While there Mr. Lincoln visited his commander and tears came to the president's eyes when he recognized the courage of Captain Worden. Later, the captain's vision was restored when the burns in his eyes healed.

The *Merrimack* continued to menace the federals' fleet of wooden ships until May of 1862 when the Confederates were forced to abandon their Navy Yard at Norfolk. Because the *Merrimack* could not be moved through shallow waters to safety the Confederates placed tons of explosives aboard the ironclad. The valuable ship was then blown to pieces before the Union could reclaim the ship for their own navy. The *Monitor* was also lost, while at sea, during a storm off Cape Hatteras, North Carolina, in December of 1862.

The battle of the ironclads is noteworthy because it signalled the end of the era when wooden ships mastered the seas. From the very moment of their historical battle the world recognized that military ships would have to be clad in iron to survive.